Nora Roberts

The Perfect Neighbour

D1136925

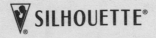

All the characters in this book have no existence outside the imagination
of the author, and have no relation whatsoever to anyone bearing the same
name or names. They are not even distantly inspired by any individual
known or unknown to the author, and all the incidents are pure invention.

Silhouette and Colophon are registered trademarks of
Harlequin Books S.A., used under licence.
Silhouette Books, Eton House, 18-24 Paradise Road,
Richmond, Surrey TW9 1SR

© Nora Roberts 1999

ISBN: 978 0 263 88528 6

026-0211

Silhouette Books' policy is to use papers that are
natural, renewable and recyclable products and made from
wood grown in sustainable forests. The logging and
manufacturing processes conform to the legal environmental regulations
of the country of origin.

Printed in the UK
by CPI Mackays, Chatham, ME5 8TD

For all my cyberpals who've touched my heart
with so many smiles.

THE MACGREGORS

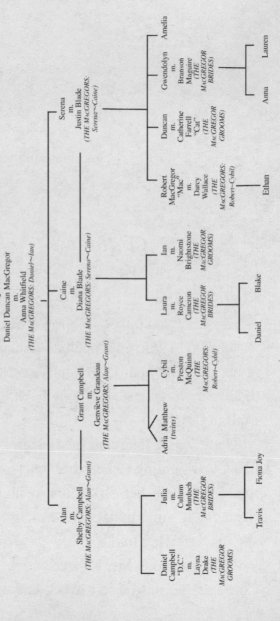

Chapter 1

"So...have you talked to him yet?"

"Hmm?" Cybil Campbell continued to work at her drawing board, diligently sectioning off the paper with the skill of long habit. "Who am I talking to?"

There was a long and gusty sigh—one that had Cybil fighting to keep her lips from twitching. She knew her first-floor neighbor Jody Myers well—and understood exactly what *him* she was referring to.

"The gorgeous Mr. Mysterious in 3B, Cyb. Come on, he moved in a week ago and hasn't said a word to anyone. But you're right across the hall. We need some details here."

"I've been pretty busy." Cybil flicked a glance up, watching Jody, with her expressive brown eyes and mop of dusky-blond hair, energetically pace around the studio. "Hardly noticed him."

Jody's first response was a snort. "Get real. You notice everything."

Jody wandered to the drawing board, hung over Cybil's shoulder, then wrinkled her nose. Nothing much interesting about a bunch of blue lines. She liked it better when Cybil started sketching in the sections.

"He doesn't even have a name on the mailbox yet. And nobody ever sees him leave the building during the day. Not even Mrs. Wolinsky, and nobody gets by her."

"Maybe he's a vampire."

"Wow." Intrigued with the idea, Jody pursed her pretty lips. "Would that be cool or what?"

"Too cool," Cybil agreed, and continued to prep her drawing, as Jody danced around the studio and chattered like a magpie.

It never bothered Cybil to have company

while she worked. The fact was, she enjoyed it. She'd never been one for isolation and quiet. It was the reason she was happy living in New York, happy to be settled into a small building with a handful of unapologetically nosy neighbors.

Such things not only satisfied her on a personal level, they were grist for her professional mill.

And of all the occupants of the old, converted warehouse, Jody Myers was Cybil's favorite. Three years earlier when Cybil had moved in, Jody had been an energetic newlywed who fervently believed that everyone should be as blissfully happy as she herself was.

Meaning, Cybil mused, married.

Now the mother of the seriously adorable eight-month-old Charlie, Jody was only more committed to her cause. And Cybil knew she herself was Jody's primary objective.

"Haven't you even run into him in the hall?" Jody wanted to know.

"Not yet." Idly, Cybil picked up a pencil, tapped it against her full-to-pouty bottom lip. Her long-lidded eyes were the green of a clear sea at twilight, and might have been exotic or sultry if they weren't almost always shimmering with humor.

"Actually, Mrs. Wolinsky's losing her touch. I have seen him leave the building during the day—which rules out vampire status."

"You have?" Instantly caught, Jody dragged a rolling stool over to the drawing board. "When? Where? How?"

"When—dawn. Where? Heading east on Grand. How? Insomnia." Getting into the spirit, Cybil swiveled on her stool. Her eyes danced with amusement. "Woke up early, and I kept thinking about the brownies left over from the party the other night."

"Atomic brownies," Jody agreed.

"Yeah, so I couldn't get back to sleep until I ate one. Since I was up anyhow, I came in here to work awhile and ended up just standing at the window. I saw him go out. You can't miss him. He must be six-four. And those shoulders..."

Both women rolled their eyes in appreciation.

"Anyway, he was carrying a gym bag and wearing black jeans and a black sweatshirt, so my deduction was he was heading to the gym to work out. You don't get those shoulders by lying around eating chips and drinking beer all day."

"Aha!" Jody speared a finger in the air. "You *are* interested."

"I'm not dead, Jody. The man is dangerously gorgeous, and you add that air of mystery along with a tight butt..." Her hands, rarely still, spread wide. "What's a girl to do but wonder?"

"Why wonder? Why don't you go knock on his door, take him some cookies or something. Welcome him to the neighborhood. Then you can find out what he does in there all day, if he's single, what he does for a living. If he's single. What—" She broke off, head lifting in alert. "That's Charlie waking up."

"I didn't hear a thing." Cybil turned her head, aiming an ear toward the doorway, listened, shrugged. "I swear, Jody, since you gave birth you have ears like a bat."

"I'm going to change him and take him for a walk. Want to come?"

"No, can't. I've got to work."

"I'll see you tonight, then. Dinner's at seven."

"Right." Cybil managed to smile as Jody dashed off to retrieve Charlie from the bedroom where she'd put him down for a nap.

Dinner at seven. With Jody's tedious and annoying cousin Frank. When, Cybil asked herself, was she going to develop a backbone and tell Jody to stop trying to fix her up?

Probably, she decided, about the same time she told Mrs. Wolinsky the same thing. And Mr. Peebles on the first floor, and her dry cleaner. What was this obsession with the people in her life to find her a man?

She was twenty-four, single and happy. Not that she didn't want a family one day. And maybe a nice house out in the burbs somewhere with a yard for the kids. And the dog. There'd have to be a dog. But that was for some time or other. She liked her life right now very much, thanks.

Resting her elbows on her drawing board, she propped her chin on her fists and gave in enough to stare out the window and allow herself to daydream. Must be spring, she mused, that was making her feel so restless and full of nervous energy.

She reconsidered going for that walk with Jody and Charlie after all but then heard her friend call out a goodbye and slam the door behind her.

So much for that.

Work, she reminded herself, and swiveled back to begin sketching in the first section of her comic strip, "Friends and Neighbors."

She had a steady and clever hand for drawing and had come by it naturally. Her mother was a successful, internationally respected artist; her father, the reclusive genius behind the long-running "Macintosh" comic strip. Together, they had given her and her siblings a love of art, a sense of the ridiculous and a solid foundation.

Cybil had known, even when she'd left the security of their home in Maine, she'd be welcomed back if New York rejected her.

But it hadn't.

For over three years now her strip had grown in popularity. She was proud of it, proud of the simplicity, warmth and humor she was able to create with everyday characters in everyday situations. She didn't attempt to mimic her father's irony or his often sharp political satires.

For her, it was life that made her laugh. Being stuck in line at the movies, finding the right pair of shoes, surviving yet another blind date.

While many saw her Emily as autobiographical, Cybil saw her as a marvelous well of ideas but never recognized the reflection. After all, Emily was a statuesque blonde who had miserable luck holding a job and worse luck with men.

Cybil herself was a brunette of average height with a successful career. As for men, well, they weren't enough of a priority for her to worry about luck one way or the other.

A scowl marred her expression, narrowing her light-green eyes as she caught herself tapping her pencil rather than using it. She just couldn't seem to concentrate. She scooped her fingers through her short cap of brandy-brown hair, pursed her softly sculpted mouth and shrugged. Maybe what she needed was a short break, a snack. Perhaps a little chocolate would get the juices flowing.

She pushed back, tucking her pencil behind her ear in an absentminded habit she'd been trying to break since childhood, left the sun-drenched studio and headed downstairs.

Her apartment was wonderfully open; aside from the studio space, that had been the main reason she'd snapped it up so quickly. A long service bar separated the kitchen from the living area, leaving the lower level all one area. Tall windows let in light and the street noises that had kept her awake and thrilled for weeks after her arrival in the city.

She moved well, another trait inherited from her mother. What her father called the Grandeau Grace. She had long limbs that had been suited to the ballet lessons she'd begged for as a child—then grown tired of. Barefoot, she padded into the kitchen, opened the refrigerator and considered.

She could whip something interesting up, she mused. She'd had cooking lessons, too—and hadn't become bored with them until she'd outdistanced her instructor in creativity.

Then she heard it and sighed. The music carried through the old walls, across the short hallway outside her door. Sad and sexy, she mused, the quiet sob of the alto sax. Mr. Mysterious in

3B didn't play every day, but she'd come to wish he would.

It always stirred her, those long liquid notes and the swirl of emotion behind them.

A struggling musician? she wondered. Hoping to find his break in New York. Brokenhearted, no doubt, she continued, weaving one of her scenarios for him as she began to take out ingredients. A woman behind it, of course. Some cold-blooded redhead who'd caught him under her spell, stripped his soul, then crushed his still-throbbing heart under her four-inch Italian heel.

A few days before, she'd invented a different lifestyle for him, one where he'd run away from his filthy rich and abusive family as a boy of sixteen. Had survived on the streets by playing on street corners in New Orleans—one of her favorite cities—then had worked his way north as that same vicious family—headed by an insane uncle—scoured the country for him.

She hadn't quite worked out why they were scouring, but it wasn't really important. He was on the run and comforted only by his music.

Or he was a government agent working undercover.

An international jewel thief, hiding from a government agent.

A serial killer trolling for his next victim.

She laughed at herself, then looked down at the ingredients she'd lined up without thinking. Whatever he was, she realized with another laugh, apparently it looked like she was making him those cookies.

His name was Preston McQuinn. He wouldn't have considered himself particularly mysterious. Just private. It was that ingrained need for privacy that had plopped him down in the heart of one of the world's busiest cities.

Temporarily, he mused, as he slipped his sax back into its case. Just temporarily. In another couple of months, the rehab would be completed on his house on Connecticut's rocky coast. Some called it his fortress, and that was fine with him. A man could be blissfully alone for weeks at a time in a fortress. And no one got in unless the gates were lifted.

He started back upstairs, leaving behind the

nearly empty living room. He only used it to play—the acoustics were dandy—or to work out if he didn't feel like going to the gym a couple of blocks away.

The second floor was where he lived—temporarily, he thought again. And all he needed in this way station was a bed, a dresser, the right lighting and a desk sturdy enough to hold his laptop, monitor and the paperwork that they often generated.

He wouldn't have had a phone, but his agent had forced a cell phone on him and had pleaded with him to keep it on.

He did—unless he didn't feel like it.

Preston sat at the desk, pleased that the little turn with his sax had cleared out the cobwebs. Mandy, his agent, was busy chewing on her inch-long nails over the progress of his latest play. He could have told her to spare the enamel. It would be done when it was done, and not a minute before.

The trouble with success, he thought, was that it became its own entity. Once you did something people liked, they wanted you to do it again—only faster and bigger. Preston didn't give a damn about what people wanted. They could break down the doors of the theater to see his next play, give him another Pulitzer, toss him another Tony and bring him money by the truckloads. Or they could stay away in droves, critically bomb the work and demand their money back.

It was the work that mattered. And it only had to matter to him.

Financially, he was secure, always had been. Mandy said that was part of his problem. Without the need or desire for money to keep him hungry, he was arrogant and aloof from his audience. Then again, she also said that was what made him a genius. Because he simply didn't give a damn.

He sat in the big room, a tall, muscular man with disordered hair the color of a well-fed mink's pelt. Eyes of cool blue scanned the words already typed. His mouth was firm and unsmiling, his face narrow, rawboned and carelessly handsome.

He tuned out the street sounds that seemed to batter against the windows day and night, and let himself slip back into the soul of the man he'd created inside the clever little computer. A man struggling desperately to survive his own desires.

The harsh sound of his buzzer made him swear as he felt himself sucked back into that empty room. He considered snarling and waiting it out, then weighed in human nature and decided the intruder would probably keep coming back until he dispatched them once and for all.

Probably the eagle-eyed old woman from the ground floor, Preston decided as he started down. She'd already tried to snag him twice when he'd headed out to the club in the evening. He was good at evading, but it was becoming a nuisance. Smarter to hit her face-on with a few rude remarks and let her huff away to gossip about him.

But when he checked the peephole, he didn't see the tidy woman with her bright bird's eyes, but a pretty brunette with hair short as a boy's and big green eyes.

From across the hall, he realized, and wondered what the hell she could want. He'd figured since she'd left him alone for nearly a week, she intended to keep right on doing so. Which made her, in his mind, the perfect neighbor.

Annoyed that she'd spoiled it, he opened the door, leaned against it. "Yeah?"

"Hi." Oh, yes, indeed, Cybil thought, he was even better when you got a good close-up look at the face. "I'm Cybil Campbell. 3A?" She offered a bright, friendly smile and gestured to her own door.

He only lifted an intriguingly winged eyebrow. "Yeah?"

A man of few words, she decided and continued to smile—though she wished his eyes would flicker away just long enough for her to crane her neck and see beyond him into the apartment. She couldn't very well try it when he was focused on her, without appearing to be prying. Which, of course, she wasn't. Really.

"I heard you playing a while ago. I work at home and sound travels."

If she was here to bitch about the noise, she was out of luck, Preston mused. He played when he felt like playing. He continued to study her coolly—the pert, slightly turned-up nose; the sensuously ripe mouth; the long narrow feet with sassily painted pink toes.

"I usually forget to turn the stereo on while I'm working," she went on cheerfully, making him notice a tiny dimple that winked off and on beside her mouth. "So it's nice to hear you play. Ralph and Sissy were into Vivaldi big-time. Which is fine, really, but monotonous when that's all you hear. They used to live in your place, Ralph and Sissy," she explained, waving a hand toward his apartment. "They moved to White Plains after Ralph had an affair with a clerk at Saks. Well, he didn't really have an affair, but he was thinking about it, and Sissy said it was move out of the city or she'd scalp him in a divorce. Mrs. Wolinsky gives them six months, but I don't know, I think they might make it. Anyway…"

She held out the pretty yellow plate with a small mountain of chocolate-chip cookies heaped on it, covered by clear pink plastic wrap. "I brought you some cookies."

He glanced down at them, giving her a very brief window of opportunity to sneak a peek around him and see his empty living room.

The poor guy couldn't even afford a couch, she thought. Then his unsmiling blue eyes flicked back to hers.

"Why?"

"Why what?"

"Why did you bring me cookies?"

"Oh, well, I was baking them. Sometimes I cook to clear out my head when I can't seem to concentrate on work. Most often it's baking that does it for me. And if I keep them all, I'll just eat them all and hate myself." The dimple kept fluttering. "Don't you like cookies?"

"I've got nothing against them."

"Well then, enjoy." She pushed them into his hands. "And welcome to the building. If you need anything I'm usually around." Again she gestured vaguely with pretty, slim-fingered hands. "And if you want to find out who's who around here, I can fill you in. I've lived here a few years now, and I know everybody."

"I won't." He stepped back and shut the door in her face.

Cybil stood where she was a moment, stunned speechless by the abrupt dismissal. She was fairly certain that she'd lived for twenty-four years without ever having had a door shut in her face, and now that she'd had the experience, she decided she didn't care for it.

She caught herself before she could pound on his door and demand her cookies back. She wouldn't sink that low, she told herself, turning sharply on her heel and marching back to her own door.

Now she knew the mysterious Mr. Mysterious was insanely attractive, built like a god and as rude as a cranky two-year-old who needed a swat on the butt and a nap. Well, that was fine, just fine. She could stay out of his way.

She didn't slam her door—figuring he'd hear it and smirk with that go-to-hell mouth of his. But when she was safely inside, she turned to the door and indulged in a juvenile exhibition of making faces, sticking out her tongue and wagging her fingers from her ears.

It made her feel marginally better.

But the bottom line was the man had her cookies, her favorite dessert plate, her very rare animosity. And she still didn't know his name.

Preston didn't regret his actions. Not for a minute. He calculated his studied rudeness would keep his terminally pert neighbor with the turned-up nose and sexy pink toenails out of his hair during his stay across the hall. The last thing he needed was the local welcoming committee rolling up at his door, especially when it was led by a bubbly motormouth brunette with eyes like a fairy.

Damn it, in New York, people were supposed to ignore their neighbors. He was pretty sure it was a city ordinance, and if not, it should be.

Just his luck, he thought, that she was single—he had no doubt that if she'd had a husband she'd have poured out all his virtues and delights. That she worked at home and would therefore be easy to trip over whenever he headed out was just another black mark.

And that she made, hands-down, the best chocolate-chip cookies in the known universe was close to unforgivable.

He'd managed to ignore them while he worked. Preston McQuinn could ignore a nuclear holocaust if the words were pumping. But when he surfaced, he started to think about them lying in his kitchen on their chirpy yellow plate.

He thought about them while he showered,

while he dressed, while he eased out the kinks brought on by hours sitting in one spot with posture his third-grade teacher, Sister Mary Joseph, had termed deplorable.

So when he went down for what he considered a well-earned beer, he eyed the plate on the counter. He'd popped the top, took a thoughtful drink. So what if he had a couple? he mused. Tossing them in the trash wasn't necessary— he'd given perky Cybil the heave-ho.

She was going to want her party plate back, he imagined. He might as well sample the wares before he dumped the plate outside her door.

So he ate one. Grunted in approval. Ate a second and blew out a breath of pure appreciation.

And when he'd consumed nearly two dozen, he cursed.

Like a damn drug, he thought, feeling slightly ill and definitely sluggish. He stared at the near-empty plate with a combination of self-disgust and greed. With what scraps of willpower he had left, he dumped the remaining cookies in a plastic bowl, then crossed the room to get his sax.

He was going to walk around the block a few times before he headed to the club.

When he opened the door he heard her stomping up the stairs. Wincing, he drew back, leaving his door open only a crack. He could hear that mile-a-minute voice of hers going, which had him lifting a brow when he saw she was alone.

"Never again," she muttered. "I don't care if she sticks bamboo shoots under my nails, holds a hot poker to my eye. I will never, ever, go through that torture again in this lifetime. That's it. Over, done."

She'd changed her clothes, Preston noted, and was wearing snug black pants with a tailored black blazer, offsetting them with a shirt the color of ripe strawberries and long dangles at her ears.

She kept talking to herself as she opened a purse the size of a postage stamp. "Life's too short to be bored witless for two precious hours of it. She will not do this to me again. I know how to say no. I just have to practice, that's all. Where the bloody hell are my keys?"

The sound of the door opening behind her

made her jump, spin around. Preston noted that the dangles in her ears didn't match and wondered if it was a fashion statement or carelessness. Since she apparently couldn't find her keys in a bag smaller than the palm of his hand, he opted for the latter.

She looked flushed, flustered and fresh. And smelled even better than her cookies. And because he noticed, she only irritated him more.

"Hold on," he said simply, then turned back into his apartment to get her plate.

Cybil had no intention of holding on, and finally found her key where it had decided to hide in the narrow inner pocket of the bag— where she'd put it so she'd know just where it was when she needed it.

But he beat her. He strode out of his apartment, letting the door slam at his back. He carried his saxophone case in one hand and her plate in the other.

"Here." He wasn't going to ask her what had put that sulky look on her sea-fairy face. He had no doubt that she'd tell him, for the next half hour.

"You're welcome," she snapped, snatching it

from him. Because her head was throbbing after two hours of listening to Jody's cousin Frank's monotone account of the vagaries of the stock market, she decided she'd give Mr. Mysterious a piece of her mind while the mood was on her.

"Look, buddy, you don't want to be friends, that's just fine. I don't need any more friends," she said, swinging the plate for emphasis. "I have so many now I can't take another on until one moves out of the country. But there's no excuse for behaving like a snot, either. All I did was introduce myself and give you some damn cookies."

His lips wanted to twitch, but he controlled it. "Damn good cookies," he said before he could stop himself, then immediately regretted it as the temper in her eyes switched to amusement.

"Oh, really?"

"Yeah." He walked away, leaving her reluctantly intrigued and completely baffled.

So she followed impulse, one of her favorite hobbies. After unlocking her door quickly, she stuck the plate on the table inside, locked up again, then, trying to keep her footsteps muffled, set off to follow him.

It would be a great strip gag for Emily, she thought, and handled right could play out for weeks.

Of course she'd have to make Emily wild about the guy, Cybil decided as she tried to tip-toe and race down the steps at the same time. It wouldn't just be normal, perfectly acceptable curiosity but dreamy-eyed obsession.

Breathless with the excitement of the chase, her mind whirling with possibilities, Cybil rushed out the front door, looked quickly right and left.

He was already halfway down the block. Long stride, she thought, and, grinning, started after him.

Emily, of course, would be sort of skulking, then jumping behind lampposts; or flattening herself against walls in case he turned around and—

Nearly yelping, Cybil jumped behind a lamp-post as the object of the chase sent an absent glance over his shoulder. With a hand over her heart, Cybil dared a peek and watched him turn the corner.

Annoyed that she'd worn heels instead of

flats to dinner, she sucked in a breath and made the dash to the corner.

He walked for twenty minutes, until her feet were screaming and her initial rush of excitement was draining fast. Did the man just wander the streets with his saxophone every night? she wondered.

Maybe he wasn't just rude. Maybe he was crazy. He'd been recently released from the asylum—that's why he didn't know how to relate to people in the normal way.

His filthy rich and abusive family had caught him, locked him up so that he couldn't claim his rightful inheritance from his beloved grandmother—who had died under suspicious circumstances and had left him her entire fortune. And all those years of being imprisoned by the corrupt psychiatrist had warped his mind.

Yes, that would be exactly what Emily would cook up in her head—and she'd be certain her tender care, her unqualified love, would cure him. Then all the friends and neighbors would try to talk her out of it—even as she dragged them into her schemes.

And before it was over Mr. Mysterious would—

She pulled up short as he walked into a small, dingy club called Delta's.

Finally, she thought, and skimmed back her hair. Now all she had to do was slip inside, find a dark corner and see what happened next.

Chapter 2

The place smelled of whiskey and smoke. Not really offensive, Cybil thought. More...atmospheric. It was dimly lit, with a pale-blue light illuminating a stingy stage. Round tables hardly bigger than pie plates were crammed together, and though most of them were occupied, the noise level was muted.

She decided people talked in whispers in such places, planning liaisons, affairs, or enjoying those already made.

At a thick wooden bar on the side wall, patrons loitered on stools and huddled over their drinks as if protecting the contents from invaders.

It was, she decided, the kind of club that belonged in a black-and-white movie from the forties. The kind where the heroine wore long, slinky dresses, dark-red lipstick with a sweep of her platinum hair falling sulkily over her left eye as she stood on the stage under a single key light, torching her way through songs about the men who'd done her wrong.

And while she did, the man who wanted her, and had done her wrong, brooded into his whiskey with his world-weary eyes shadowed by the brim of his fedora.

In other words, she thought with a smile, it was perfect.

Hoping to go unnoticed, she scooted along the rear wall and found a table and, sitting, watched him through a haze of smoke and whiskey fumes.

He wore black. Jeans with a T-shirt tucked into the waistband. He'd already taken off the leather jacket he'd put on against the evening chill. The woman he was speaking with was gorgeous, black and outfitted in a hot red jumpsuit that hugged every curvaceous inch. She had to be six feet tall, Cybil mused, and when she threw back her beautiful head and laughed, the full rich sound rocked through the room.

For the first time Cybil saw him smile. No, not just smile, she thought, transfixed by the lightning transformation of that stern and handsome face. That hot punch of grin, the hammerblow power of it, couldn't be called anything as tame as a smile.

It was full of fun and affection and sly humor. It made her rest her chin on her fisted hands and grin in response.

She imagined he and the beautiful Amazon were lovers, was certain of it when the woman grabbed his face in her hands and kissed him lavishly. Of course, Cybil thought, a man like that—with all those secrets and heartaches—would have an exotic lover, and they would meet in a dim, smoky bar where the music was dreamy and sad.

Finding it wonderfully romantic, she sighed.

Onstage, Delta gave Preston's cheeks an affectionate pinch. "So now you got women following you, sugar lips?"

"She's a lunatic."

"You want me to bounce her out?"

"No." He didn't glance back but could feel those big green eyes on him. "I'm pretty sure she's a harmless lunatic."

Delta's tawny eyes glittered with amusement. "Then I'll just check her out. Woman starts stalking my sugar lips, I gotta see what's she made of, right, André?"

The skinny black man at the piano stopped noodling keys long enough to smile up at her out of a face as battered and worn as the old spinet he played. "That you do, Delta. Don't hurt her, now—she's just a little thing. You ready to blow?" he asked Preston.

"You start. I'll catch up."

As Delta glided offstage, André's long, narrow fingers began to make magic. Preston let the mood of it slide into him; then, closing his eyes, let the music come.

It took him away. It cleared his head of the words and the people and the scenes that often crowded his head. When he played like this, there was nothing but the music, and the aching pleasure of making it.

He'd once told Delta it was like sex. It dragged something out of you, put something back. And when it was over, it was always too soon.

In the back, Cybil drifted into it, slid down into those low, bluesy notes, rose up with the sudden wailing sobs. It was different, she thought, watching him play than just hearing it through the walls. Watching him, there was more power, more heartbreak, more of that subtle sexual pull.

It was music to weep by. To make love to. To dream on.

It caught her, focused her on the stage so she didn't see Delta moving toward her table.

"What's your pleasure, little sister?"

"Hmm." Distracted, Cybil glanced up, smiled vaguely. "It's wonderful. The music. It makes my heart hurt."

Delta lifted a brow. The girl had a bright and pretty face, she mused. Didn't look much like a lunatic with that tipped nose and those long-lidded eyes. "You drinking or just taking up space?"

"Oh." Of course, Cybil realized, a place

like this needed to sell drinks. "It's whiskey music," she said with another smile. "I'll have a whiskey."

Delta's brow only arched higher. "You don't look old enough to be ordering whiskey, little sister."

Cybil didn't bother to sigh. It was an opinion she heard constantly. She flipped open her purse, pulled out her driver's license.

Delta took it, studied it. "All right, Cybil Angela Campbell, I'll get your whiskey."

"Thanks." Content, Cybil rested her chin on her fists again and just listened. It surprised her when Delta came back not with one glass of whiskey but two, then folded that glamorous body into the chair next to her.

"So, what are you doing in a place like this, young Cybil? You got a Rainbow Room face."

Cybil opened her mouth, then realized she could hardly say she'd followed her mysterious neighbor all over Soho. "I don't live far from here. I suppose I just followed an impulse." She lifted the whiskey, gestured with it to the stage. "I'm glad I did," she said, then drank.

Delta's lips pursed. The girl might look like

a varsity cheerleader, but she drank her whiskey like a man. "You go wandering around the streets alone at night, somebody's going to eat you up, little sister."

Cybil's eyes gleamed over the rim of her glass. "Oh, I don't think so. Big sister."

Considering, Delta nodded. "Maybe, maybe not. Delta Pardue." She touched her glass to Cybil's. "This is my place."

"I like your place, Delta."

"Maybe, maybe not." Delta let loose that rich laugh again. "But you sure like my man there. You've had your pretty cat's-eyes on him since you came in."

Thoughtfully, Cybil swirled her whiskey while she debated how to play it. Though she had no doubt she could handle herself on the streets—or anywhere else, for that matter—Delta outweighed her by at least thirty pounds. And as she'd said, it was her place. Her man. No point in making a potential new friend want to rip out her lungs at their first meeting.

"He's very attractive," Cybil said casually. "It's hard not to look. So I'll keep looking if it's all the same to you. I doubt his eyes are going

to wander when he's got someone like you in
focus."

Delta's teeth flashed in a brilliant grin.
"Maybe you can take care of yourself after all.
You're a smart girl, aren't you?"

Cybil chuckled into her whiskey. "Oh, yeah.
I am. And I do like your place. I like it a lot.
How long have you owned it, Delta?"

"This? Two years here."

"And before? It's New Orleans I'm hearing in
your voice, isn't it?"

Delta inclined her head. "You got good
ears."

"I do, actually, for dialects, but yours is one
I couldn't miss. I have family in New Orleans.
My mother grew up there."

"I don't know any Campbells—what's your
mama's maiden name?"

"Grandeau."

Delta eased back. "I know Grandeaus, many
Grandeaus. Are you kin to Miss Adelaide?"

"Great-aunt."

"Grand lady."

Cybil snorted, drank. "Stuffy, irritating and
cold as winter. The twins and I—my brother

and sister—used to think she was a witch of the wicked sort."

"She has power, but it only comes from money and a name. Grandeau, eh? Who's your mama?"

"GenviÈve Grandeau Campbell, the artist."

"Miss Gennie." Delta set her whiskey down so that she could rear back and thump a hand to her heart as she rocked with laughter. "Miss Gennie's little girl comes into my place. Oh, the world is a wonderful thing."

"You know my mother?"

"My mama cleaned house for your *grand-mÈre,* little sister."

"Mazie? You're Mazie's daughter? Oh." Instantly bonded, Cybil grabbed Delta's hand. "My mother talked about Mazie all the time. We visited her once when I was a little girl. She gave us beignets, fresh and wonderful. We sat on the front porch and had lemonade, and my father did a sketch of her."

"She put it in her parlor and was very proud. I was in the city when your family came. I was working. My mama, she talked of that visit for weeks after. She had a place deep in her heart for Miss Gennie."

"Wait until I tell them I met you. How is your mother, Delta?"

"She died last year."

"Oh." Cybil laid her other hand over Delta's, cupping it warmly. "I'm so sorry."

"She lived a good life, died sleeping, so died a good death. Your mama and your daddy, they came to the funeral. They sat in the church. They stood at the grave. You come from good people, young Cybil."

"Yes, I do. So do you."

Preston didn't know how to figure it. There was Delta, a woman he considered the most sane of anyone he knew, huddled together with the pretty crazy woman, apparently already the fastest of friends. Sharing whiskey, laughs. Holding hands the way women do.

For more than an hour they sat together in the back of the room. Now and then, Cybil would begin what could only have been one of her chattering monologues, her hands gesturing, her face mobile. Delta would lean back and laugh, or lean forward, shaking her head in amazement.

"Look at that, André." Preston leaned on the piano.

André wiggled his fingers loose, then lit a cigarette. "Like a couple of hens in the coop. That's a pretty girl there, my man. Got sparkle to her."

"I hate sparkle," Preston muttered, and no longer in the mood to play, tucked his sax in the case. "Catch you next time."

"I'll be here."

He thought he should just walk out, but he was just a little irritated to have his good friend getting chummy with his lunatic. Besides, it would give him some satisfaction to let his nosy neighbor know he was onto her.

But when he stopped by the table, Cybil only glanced up and smiled at him. "Hi. Aren't you going to play anymore? It was wonderful."

"You followed me."

"I know. It was rude. But I'm so glad I did. I loved listening, and I might never have met Delta otherwise. We were just—"

"Don't do it again," he said shortly, and stalked to the door.

"Ooooh, he's plenty pissed off," Delta said with a chuckle. "Got that ice in his eyes, chills down to bone."

"I should apologize," Cybil said as she bolted to her feet. "I don't want him angry with you."

"Me? He's—"

"I'll come back soon." She dropped a kiss on Delta's cheek, making the woman blink in surprise. "Don't worry, I'll smooth things over."

When she dashed out, Delta simply stared after her, then let out one of her long laughs. "Little sister, you got no idea what you're in for. Then again," she mused, "neither does sugar lips."

Outside, Cybil dashed down the sidewalk. "Hey!" she shouted at his retreating back, then cursed herself for not having the sense to ask Delta what the man's name was. "Hey!" Risking a twisted ankle, she switched from jog to run and managed to catch up.

"I'm sorry," she began, tugging on the sleeve of his jacket. "Really. It's completely my fault."

"Who said it wasn't?"

"I shouldn't have followed you. It was impulse. I have such a problem resisting impulse— always have—and I was irritated because of that idiot Frank and…well, that doesn't matter. I only wanted to—could you slow down a little?"

"No."

Cybil rolled her eyes. "All right, all right, you wish I'd get run over by a truck, but there's no need to be upset with Delta. We just started talking and we found out that her mother used to work for my grandmother, and she—Delta, I mean—knows my parents and some of my Grandeau cousins, so we hit it off."

He did stop now, to simply stare at her. "Of all the gin joints in all the towns in all the world," he muttered, and made her laugh.

"I had to follow you into that one and make pals with your girlfriend. Sorry."

"My girlfriend? Delta?"

And to Cybil's amazement, the man could laugh. Really laugh, with a wonderful baritone rumble that melted all the ice and made her sigh in delight.

"Does Delta look like anyone's *girl*friend? Man, you are from Mars."

"It's just an expression. I didn't want to be presumptive and call her your lover."

His eyes were still warm with amusement as he stared down at her. "That's a happy thought, kid, but the guy I was just jamming with happens to be her husband, and a friend of mine."

"The skinny man at the piano? Really?" Pursing her lips, Cybil thought about it, found it charming and romantic. "Isn't that lovely?"

Preston only shook his head and started walking again.

"What I meant was," Cybil continued—he'd just known she couldn't possibly be finished—as she hurried along beside him, "I'm sure she came back to check me out, you know? To make sure I wasn't going to hassle you, and then, well, one thing led to another. I don't want you to be annoyed with her."

"I'm not annoyed with her. You, on the other hand, have gone so far beyond being an annoyance I can't find the word."

Her mouth fell into a pout. "Well, I'm sorry, and I'll certainly make it a point to leave you alone, since that's apparently what you like best."

Her perky nose went up in the air, and she sailed across the street in the opposite direction from their building.

Preston stood there a moment, watching her scissor those very pretty legs down the opposite sidewalk. Then, with a shrug, he turned the corner, telling himself he was glad to be rid of her. It wasn't his concern if she wandered around alone at night. She wouldn't have been out walking around on those silly, skinny heels if she hadn't followed him in the first place.

He wasn't going to worry about it.

And swearing, he turned around, headed back. He was going to make sure she got home, that was all. Back inside, where he could wash any responsibility for her welfare off his hands and forget her.

He was still the best part of a crosstown block away when he saw it happen. The man slid out of the shadows, made his grab and had Cybil letting out an ear-piercing scream as she struggled. Preston dumped his case, sprinted forward with his fists already clenched.

Then skidded to an amazed halt as Cybil not only broke free but doubled her attacker over with a hard knee to the groin, knocked him flat with a perfect uppercut.

"I only had ten lousy dollars in here. Ten lousy dollars, you jerk!" She was shouting by the time Preston gathered his wits and rushed up beside her. "If you'd needed money, why didn't you just ask!"

"You hurt?"

"Yes, damn it. And it's your fault. I wouldn't have hit him so hard if I hadn't been mad at you."

Noting that she was nursing the knuckles on her right hand, Preston grabbed it by the wrist. "Let's see. Wiggle your fingers."

"Go away."

"Come on, wiggle."

"Hey!" The shout came from a woman hanging out an open window across the street. "You want I should call the cops?"

"Yes." Cybil snapped the word back as she wiggled her fingers and Preston probed, then blew out a steadying breath. "Yes, please. Thanks."

"Polite little victim, aren't you?" Preston muttered. "Nothing's broken. You might want to get it x-rayed anyway."

"Thanks so much, Dr. Doom." She jerked a hand away, kept her chin lifted and gestured with her uninjured hand in what Preston thought of as a grandly regal gesture. "You can go. I'm just fine."

As the man sprawled on the sidewalk began to moan and stir, Preston set a foot on his throat. "I think I'll just stick around. Why don't you go get my sax for me. I dropped it back there when I still believed the Big Bad Wolf ate Red Riding Hood."

She nearly told him to go get it himself, then decided if she had to hit the jerk on the sidewalk again, she'd hurt herself as much as him. With stiff dignity, she walked down the block, picked up the case and carried it back.

"Thank you," she said.

"For what?"

"For the thought."

"Don't mention it." Preston added a bit more weight when the man on the ground began to curse.

When the squad car pulled up ten minutes later, he stepped back. Cybil wasn't having any trouble giving the cops the details, and Preston harbored the hope that he could just slide away and stay out of it. The hope died as one of the uniforms turned to him.

"Did you see what happened here?"

Preston sighed. "Yeah."

And that was why it was nearly 2 a.m. before he trooped up the steps with Cybil toward their respective apartments. He still had the unappealing taste of police station coffee in his mouth and a low-grade headache on the brew.

"It was kind of exciting, wasn't it? All those cops and bad guys. It was hard to tell one from the other in the detective bureau. Well, you could because the detectives have to wear ties. I wonder why. It was nice of them to show me around. You should have come. The interrogation rooms look just the way you imagine they would. Dark and creepy."

He was certain she had to be the only person on the planet who could find a sunny side to being mugged.

"I'm wired," she announced. "Aren't you wired? Want some cookies? I still have plenty."

He nearly ignored her as he dug out his keys, then his stomach reminded him he hadn't eaten anything for the past eight hours. And her cookies were a minor miracle.

"Maybe."

"Great." She unlocked her door, left it open, stepping out of her shoes as she walked to the kitchen. "You can come in," she called out. "I'll put them on a plate for you so you can take them back and eat them in your own den, but there's no point in waiting in the hall."

He stepped in, leaving the door open behind him. He should have known her place would be bright and cheerful, full of cute and classy little accents. With his hands in his pockets, he wandered around, tuning out her bubbling chatter while she transferred cookies from a canister in the shape of a manically grinning cow to the same bright-yellow plate she'd used before.

"You talk too much."

"I know." She skimmed a hand over her spiky bangs. "Especially when I'm nervous or wired up."

"Are you ever otherwise?"

"Now and then."

He noted a scatter of framed photos, several pairs of earrings, another shoe, a romance novel and the scent of apple blossoms. Each suited her, he thought, as perfectly as the next. Then he paused in front of a framed copy of a comic strip on the wall.

"Friends and Neighbors," he mused, then studied the signature under the last section. It read simply, Cybil. "This you?"

She glanced over. "Yes. That's my strip. I don't imagine you spend much time reading the comics, do you?"

Knowing a dig when he heard one, he looked back over his shoulder. It must have been the late hour, he decided, after a long day that made her look so fresh and pretty and appealing. "Grant Campbell—'Macintosh'—that your old man?"

"He's not old, but yes, he's my father."

The Campbells, Preston mused, meant the MacGregors. And wasn't that a coincidence? He moved over to stand on the opposite side of the counter and help himself to the cookies she was arranging in a stylish circular pattern.

"I like the edge to his work."

"I'm sure he'll appreciate that." Because he was reaching for another cookie, Cybil smiled. "Want some milk?"

"No. Got a beer?"

"With cookies?" She grimaced but turned to her refrigerator. Preston had a chance to see it was well stocked as she bent down—which gave him a chance to appreciate just what snug black slacks could do for a perky woman's excellent butt—and retrieved a bottle of Beck's Dark.

"This do? It's what Chuck likes."

"Chuck has good taste. Boyfriend?"

She smirked, getting out a pilsner glass before he could tell her he'd just take the bottle. "I suppose that indicates that I'm the type to have *boy*friends, but no. He's Jody's husband. Jody and Chuck Myers, just below you in 2B. I was out to dinner with them tonight, and Jody's excessively boring cousin Frank."

"Is that what you were muttering about when you came home?"

"Was I muttering?" She frowned, then leaned

on the counter and ate one of his cookies. Muttering was another habit she kept trying to break. "Probably. It's the third time Jody's roped me into a date with Frank. He's a stockbroker. Thirty-five, single, handsome if you like that lantern-jawed, chiseled-brow sort. He drives a BMW coupe, has an apartment on the Upper East Side, a summer place in the Hamptons, wears Armani suits, enjoys French-provincial cuisine and has perfect teeth."

Amused despite himself, Preston washed down cookies with cold beer. "So why aren't you married and looking for a nice split-level in Westchester?"

"Ah, you've just voiced my friend Jody's dream. And I'll tell you why." She wagged a cookie, then bit in. "One, I don't want to get married or move to Westchester. Two, and really more to the point, I would rather be strapped to an anthill than strapped to Frank."

"What's wrong with him?"

"He bores me," she said, then winced. "That's so unkind."

"Why? Sounds honest to me."

"It is honest." She picked up another cookie,

ate it with only a little guilt. "He's really a very nice man, but I don't think he's read a book in the last five years or seen a movie. A few selected films, perhaps, but not a movie. Then he critiques them."

"I don't even know him, and I'm already bored."

That made her laugh and reach for another cookie. "He's been known to check out his grooming in the back of his spoon at the dinner table—just to make sure he's still perfect—and he can spend the rest of his life, and yours, talking about annuities and stock futures. And all that aside, he kisses like a fish."

"Really." He forgot he'd wanted to grab a handful of cookies and get out. "And how is that exactly?"

"You know." She made an *O* with her mouth, then laughed. "You can imagine how a fish kisses, which I suppose they don't, but if they did. I nearly escaped without having the experience tonight, then Jody got in the way."

"And it doesn't occur to you to say no?"

"Of course it occurs to me." Her grin was quick and completely self-deprecating. "I just can't seem to get it out in time. Jody loves me, and for reasons that continue to elude me, she loves Frank. She's sure we'd make a wonderful couple. You know how it is when someone you care about puts that kind of benign pressure on you."

"No. I don't."

She tilted her head. Remembering his empty living room. No furniture, and now no family. "That's too bad. As inconvenient as it may be from time to time, I wouldn't trade it for anything."

"How's the hand?" he asked when he saw her rubbing her knuckles.

"Oh. A little sore still. It'll probably give me some trouble working tomorrow. But I should be able to turn the experience into a good strip."

"I can't see Emily laying a mugger out on his ass."

Cybil's face glowed on a grin. "You *do* read it."

"Now and again." She was entirely too pretty, he thought suddenly. Entirely too bright. And it was abruptly too tempting to find out if she tasted the same way.

That's what happened, Preston supposed, when you hung around eating homemade cookies in the middle of the night with a woman who made her living looking at the light side of life.

"You don't have your father's edge or your mother's artistic genius, but you have a nice little talent for the absurd."

She let out a half laugh. "Well, thank you so much for that unsolicited critique."

"No problem." He picked up the plate. "Thanks for the cookies."

She narrowed her eyes as he headed for the door. Well, he was going to see just how much of a talent she had for the absurd in some upcoming strips, she decided.

"Hey."

He paused, glanced back. "Hey, what?"

"You got a name, apartment 3B?"

"Yeah, I've got a name, 3A. It's McQuinn." He balanced his beer and his plate, and shut the door between them.

Chapter 3

When scenes and people filled her head, Cybil could work until her fingers cramped and refused to hold pencil or brush.

She spent the next day fueled on cookies and the diet soft drinks she liked to pretend balanced out the cookie calories. On paper, section by section, Emily and her friend Cari—who over the last couple of years had taken on several Jody-like attributes—plotted and planned on how to discover the secrets of the Mr. Mysterious.

She was going to call him "Quinn," but not for several installments.

For three days she rarely left her drawing board. Jody had a key, so it wasn't necessary to run down and let her in every time she dropped over for a visit. And Jody was always happy enough to dash down to open the door for Mrs. Wolinsky or one of the other neighbors who stopped by.

At one point on the third evening, enough people were in the apartment to have put together a small, informal party while Cybil remained coloring in her big Sunday strip.

Someone had turned on the stereo. Music blared, but it didn't distract her. Laughter and conversation rose up the stairs, and there was a shout of greeting as someone else dropped in.

She smelled popcorn, and wondered idly if anyone would bring her some.

Leaning back, she studied her work. No, she didn't have her father's edge, she acknowledged, or her mother's genius. But all in all, she did indeed have a "nice little talent."

She had a quick and clever hand at drawing. She could paint—quite well, really, she mused—if the mood was right. The strip gave her an arena for her own brand of social commentary.

Perhaps she didn't dig into sore spots or turn a sarcastic pencil toward politics, but her work made people laugh. It gave them company in the morning over their hurried cup of coffee or along with a lazy Sunday breakfast.

More than anything, she thought as she signed her name, it made her happy.

If McQuinn in 3B thought his careless comment insulted her, he was wrong. She was more than content with her nice little talent.

Flushed with the success of three days' intense work, she picked up the phone as it rang and all but sang into it. "Hello?"

"Well, well, there's a cheery lass."

"Grandpa!" Cybil leaned back in her chair and stretched cramped muscles. "Yes, I'm a cheery lass, and there's no one I'd rather talk to than you."

Technically, Daniel MacGregor wasn't her grandfather, but that had never stopped either of them from thinking of him as such. Love ignored technicalities.

"Is that so? Then why haven't you called me

or your grandmother? You know how she worries about you down there in that big city all alone."

"Alone?" Amused, she held out the phone so the sounds of the party downstairs would travel through the receiver to Hyannis Port. "It doesn't feel as if I'm ever alone."

"You've got the place full of people again?"

"So it seems. How are you? How is everyone? Tell me everything."

She settled back, happy to chat with him about family, her aunts and uncles, her cousins, the babies.

She listened and laughed, added her own comments, and was pleased when he told her there was a family gathering in the works for the summer.

"Wonderful. I can't wait to see everyone again. It's been too long since Ian and Naomi's wedding last fall. I miss you."

"Well then, why do you have to wait until summer? We're right here, after all."

"Maybe I'll surprise you."

"I called with one for you. I'll wager you haven't heard as yet that little Naomi's expecting. We'll have another bairn under the Christmas tree this year."

"Oh, Grandpa, that's wonderful. I'll call them tonight. And with Darcy and Mac ready to have theirs any day, we'll have lots of babies to cuddle this Christmas."

"For a young woman so fond of babes, you ought to be busy making your own."

It was an old theme and made her grin. "But my cousins are doing such a fine job of it."

"Hah! That they are, but that doesn't mean you can shirk your duty, little girl. You may be a Campbell by birth, but you've got some MacGregor in your heart."

"Well, I could always give in and marry Frank."

"The one with the fish mouth?"

"No, he just kisses like a fish. Then again… yeah, the one with the fish mouth. We could make you some guppies."

"Bah. You need a man, not a trout in an Italian suit. A man with more on his mind than dollars and cents, with an understanding of art, with enough of a serious nature to keep you out of trouble."

"I keep myself out of trouble," she reminded him, but decided it was best not to mention the mugging incident. "Besides, Grandma won't let me have you, so I'll just have to pine away here in the big, bad city."

He let out a bark of a laugh. "All the men in that city, you ought to be able to find one to suit you. You get out and about, don't you? You're not sitting there all day writing your funny papers."

"Just lately, but I hit a hot streak here and needed to run with it. There's this new guy across the hall. Kind of surly and standoffish. No, actually, let's just say it straight. He's rude and abrupt. I think he's out of work, except he plays the sax sometimes in this little club a few blocks from here. He's just the perfect new neighbor for Emily."

"Is that so?"

"He stays inside his apartment all day, doesn't talk to anyone. His name's McQuinn."

"If he doesn't talk to anyone, how do you know his name?"

"Grandpa." She allowed herself a smug smile. "Have you ever known me to fail getting anyone to talk to me if I put my mind to it? Not that he's the chatty sort even when you prime his pump with cookies, but I wheedled his name out of him."

"And how does he look to you, little girl?"

"He looks good, very, very good. He's going to drive Emily crazy."

"Is he, now?" Daniel said, and laughed with delight.

When he'd gotten all that he needed to know out of his honorary granddaughter, Daniel made his next call. He hummed to himself, examined his nails, buffed them on his shirt, then grinned fiercely when Preston answered the phone with an impatient, "Yeah, what?"

"Ah, you've such a sweet nature to you, McQuinn. It warms my heart."

"Mr. MacGregor." There was no mistaking that booming Scottish burr. In an abrupt shift of mood, Preston smiled warmly and pushed away from his computer.

"Right you are. And how are you settling in to the apartment there?"

"Well enough. I have to thank you again for letting me use it while my house is a construction zone. I'd never have been able to work with all those people around." He scowled at the wall as the noise from across the hall battered against it. "Not that it's much better here tonight. My neighbor seems to be celebrating something."

"Cybil? She's my granddaughter, you know. Sociable child."

"You're telling me. I didn't realize she was your granddaughter."

"Well, in a roundabout way. You ought to shake yourself loose, boy, and join the party."

"No, thanks." He'd rather drink drain cleaner. "I think half the population of Soho's crammed in there. This building of yours, Mr. MacGregor, is full of people who'd rather talk than eat. Your granddaughter appears to be the leader."

"Friendly girl. It comforts me to know you're across the hall for a bit. You're a sensible sort, McQuinn. I don't mind imposing by asking you to keep an eye on her. She can be naïve, if you get my meaning. I worry about her."

Preston had the image of her flattening a mugger with the speed and precision of a lightweight boxer and smiled to himself. "I wouldn't worry."

"Well, I won't knowing you're close by. Pretty young thing like Cybil...she is a pretty thing, isn't she?"

"Cute as a button."

"Smart, too. And responsible, for all it seems like she's fluttering through life. You can't be a dim-witted flutterer and produce a popular comic strip day after day, now can you? Got to be creative, artistic and practical enough to meet deadlines. But you know about that sort of business, don't you? Writing plays isn't an easy business."

"No." Preston rubbed his eyes, gritty from fighting with work that refused to run smooth. "It's not."

"But you've a gift, McQuinn, a rare one. I admire that."

"It's been feeling like a curse lately. But I appreciate it."

"You should get yourself out, take your mind off it. Kiss a pretty girl. Not that I know much about writing—though I've two grandchildren who make their living from it, and damn well, too. You should make the most of being right there in the city before you take yourself back and lock the doors on your house."

"Maybe I will."

"Oh, and McQuinn, you'll do me the favor of not mentioning to Cybil that I asked you to mind her a bit? She'd get huffy over it. But her grandmother worries herself sick over that girl."

"She won't hear it from me," Preston promised.

Since the noise was going to drive him crazy, Preston took himself off. He played at the club but found it didn't quite get him past the thoughts that jangled in his brain.

It was too easy to imagine Cybil sitting at the table in the back, her chin on her fists, her lips curved, her eyes dreamy.

She'd invaded one of his more well-guarded vaults, and he resented it bitterly.

Delta's was one of his escapes. There were times he'd drive into the city from Connecticut just to slip onto the stage with André and play until all the tension of the day dissolved into, then out of, the music.

He could drive home again or, if the hour grew too late, just drop down on the cot in Delta's back room and sleep until morning.

No one bothered him at the club or expected more than he wanted to give.

But now that Cybil had been here, he'd started to look at that back table, and wondered if she'd slip in again. To watch him with those big green eyes.

"My man," André said as he stopped to take a long drink from the water glass he kept on his beloved piano. "You ain't just playing the blues tonight. You got 'em."

"Yeah. Looks like."

"Usually a woman tangled up there when a man's got that look about him."

Preston shook his head, scowling as he lifted the sax to his lips. "No. No woman. It's work."

André merely pursed his lips as Preston sent out music that throbbed like a pulse. "You say so, brother. If you say so."

He got home at three, prepared to beat on Cybil's door and demand quiet. It was a letdown to arrive and discover the party was over. There wasn't a sound coming from her apartment.

He let himself in, locked up, then told himself he'd take advantage of the peace. After brewing a pot of coffee strong enough to dance on, he settled back at his machine, back into his play, back into the minds of characters who were destroying their lives because they couldn't reach their own hearts.

The sun was up when he stopped, when the sudden rush of energy that had flooded him drained out again. He decided it was the first solid work he'd managed in nearly a week, and celebrated by falling facedown and fully dressed into bed.

And there he dreamed.

Of a pretty face framed by a fringe of glossy brown hair, offset by long-lidded and enormous eyes the color of willow fronds. Of a voice that bubbled like a brook.

Why does everything have to be so serious? she asked him, laughing as she slid her arms up his chest, linked them around his neck.

Because life's a serious business.

That's only one-half of one of the coins.

There are lots and lots of coins. Aren't you going to dance with me?

He already was. They were in Delta's, and though it was empty, the music was playing, low and sultry.

I'm not going to keep my eye on you. I can't afford it.

But you already are.

The top of her head reached his chin. When she tilted her head back, flicked her tongue lazily over his jaw, he felt the rush of his own blood.

That's not all you want to keep on me, is it?

I don't want you.

There was that laugh, light as air, frothy as champagne. *What's the point of lying,* she asked him, *in your own dreams? You can do anything you want to me in dreams. It won't matter.*

I don't want you, he said again, even as he pulled her to the floor.

He awoke, sweating, tangled in sheets, appalled, amazed, and finally when his head started to clear, amused.

The woman was a menace, he decided, and the only thing that had reflected any sort of reality in the painfully erotic dream was that he didn't want her.

He rubbed his hands over his face, glanced at the watch still on his wrist. Since it was after four in the afternoon, he judged he'd gotten the first decent eight hours of sleep he'd had in nearly a week. So what if it was at the wrong end of the time scale?

He trooped down to the kitchen, drank the dregs of the coffee and rooted out the only bagel that still looked edible. He was going to have to break down and buy some food.

He spent an hour working out, mechanically lifting weights, reminding his body it wasn't built to simply sit at a keyboard. Pleased that the sweat he'd worked up this time had nothing to do with sexual fantasies, he spent another twenty minutes indulging in a hot shower, and shaved for the first time in three—or maybe it was four—days.

He thought he might take himself out for a decent meal—which would be a nice change of pace. Then he'd face the tedium and low-grade horror of going to the market. Dressed and feeling remarkably clearheaded and cheerful, he opened his door.

Cybil dropped the hand she'd lifted to ring his buzzer. "Thank God you're home."

His mood wavered as his thought zoomed right back to the dream, and the barroom floor. "What?"

"You have to do me a favor."

"No, I don't."

"It's an emergency." She grabbed his arm before he could walk by. "It's life and death. My life and very possibly Mrs. Wolinsky's nephew Johnny's death. Because one of us is going to die if I have to go out with him, which is why I told her I had a date tonight."

"And you think this interests me because…"

"Oh, don't be surly now, McQuinn, I'm a desperate woman. Look, she didn't give me time to think. I'm a terrible liar. I mean, I just don't lie very often, so I'm bad at it. She kept asking who I was going out with, and I couldn't think of anybody, so I said you."

Because she'd meant it when she'd told him she was desperate, she darted in front of him to block his path.

"Kid, let me point out one simple fact. This isn't my problem."

"No, it's mine, I know it, and I would have made something better up if she hadn't caught me when I was working and thinking of something else." She lifted her hands, pushed them through her hair and had it standing in spikes. "She's going to be watching, don't you see? She's going to know if we don't go out of here together."

She whirled away to pace and rap her knuckles against her temples as if to stimulate thought. "Look, all you have to do is walk out of here with me, give an appearance of a nice, casual date. We'll go have a cup of coffee or something, spend a couple of hours, then come back—because she'll know if we don't come back together, too. She knows everything. I'll give you a hundred dollars."

That stopped him. The basic absurdity of it pulled him up short at the head of the stairs. "You'll pay me to go out with you?"

"It's not exactly like that—but close enough. I know you can use the money, and it's only fair to compensate you for your time. A hundred dollars, McQuinn, for a couple hours, and I'll buy the coffee."

He leaned back against the wall, studying her. It was just ridiculous enough to appeal to a sense of the absurd he'd all but forgotten he had. "No pie?"

Her laugh erupted on a gush of relief. "Pie? You want pie? You got pie."

"Where's the C note?"

"The...oh, the money. Hold on."

She dashed back into her apartment. He could hear her running up the steps, slamming around.

"Just let me fix myself up a little," she called out.

"Meter's running, kid."

"Okay, okay. Where the hell is my...ah! Two minutes, two minutes. I don't want her to tell me I'd hold on to a man if I'd just put on lipstick."

He had to give her credit. When she said two minutes, she meant it. She ran back out, her feet in another pair of those skinny heels, her lips slicked with deep pink and earrings dangling. Mismatched again he noted as she handed him a crisp hundred-dollar bill.

"I really appreciate this. I know how foolish it must seem. I can't stand to hurt her feelings, that's all."

"Her feelings are worth a hundred bucks to you, it's your business." Entertained, he stuffed the bill in his back pocket. "Let's go. I'm hungry."

"Oh, do you want dinner? I can spring for a meal. There's a diner just down the street. Good pasta. Okay, now. Pretend you don't know she's keeping her eye out for us," she murmured as they walked to the entrance. "Just look natural. Hold my hand, will you?"

"Why?"

"Oh, for heaven's sake." She snatched his hand, linked her fingers firmly with his, then shot him a bright smile. "We're going on a date, our first. Try to look like we're enjoying ourselves."

"You only gave me a hundred," he reminded her, surprised when she laughed.

"God, you're a hard man, 3B. A really hard man. Let's get you a hot meal and see if it improves your mood."

It did. But it would have taken a stronger

man than he to hold out against an enormous, family-style bowl of spaghetti and meatballs and Cybil's sunny disposition.

"It's great, isn't it?" She watched him plow through the food with pleasure. Poor man, she thought, probably hasn't had a decent meal in weeks. "I always eat too much when I come here. They give you enough for six starving teenagers with each serving. Then I end up taking home the rest and eating too much the next day. You can save me from that and take mine home with you."

"Fine." He topped off their glasses of Chianti.

"You know, I bet there are dozens of clubs downtown that would be thrilled to hire you to play."

"Huh?"

"Your sax."

She smiled at him, luring him to look at her mouth, that flickering dimple, and wonder again.

"You're so good. I can't imagine you won't find steady work really soon."

Amused, he lifted his wine. She thought he

was an out-of-work musician. Fine, then. Why not? "Gigs come and they go."

"Do you work private parties?" Inspired, she leaned on the table. "I know a lot of people—someone's always having a party."

"I bet they are, in your little world."

"I could give your name out if you like. Do you mind traveling?"

"Where am I going?"

"Some of my relatives own hotels. Atlantic City's not far. I don't suppose you have a car."

He had a snazzy new Porsche stored in a downtown garage. "Not on me."

She laughed, nibbled on bread. "Well, it's not difficult to get from New York to Atlantic City."

As entertaining as it was, he thought it wise to steer off awhile. "Cybil, I don't need anyone to manage my life."

"Terrible habit of mine." Unoffended, she broke the bread in half and offered him part. "I get involved. Then I'm annoyed when other people do the same to me. Like Mrs. Wolinsky, the current president of Let's Find Cybil a Nice Young Man Club. It drives me crazy."

"Because you don't want a nice young man."

"Oh, I suppose I will, eventually. Coming from a big family sort of predisposes you—or me, anyway—into wanting one of your own. But there's lots of time for that. I like living in the city, doing what I want when I want. I'd hate to keep regular hours, which is why nothing ever stuck before cartooning. Not that it isn't work or doesn't take discipline, but it's my work and my time. Like your music, I guess."

"I guess." His work was very rarely a pleasure—as hers seemed to be. But his music was.

"McQuinn." Smiling, she nudged her bowl to the side, thinking it would make him a very nice meal later in the week. "How often do you really rip loose and come up with more than, oh, say, three declarative sentences in a row during a conversation?"

He ate the last half of his last meatball, studied her. "I like November. I talk a lot in November. It's the kind of transitory month that makes me feel philosophical."

"Three on the button, and clever, too." She

laughed at him. "You have a sly sense of humor in there, don't you?" Sitting back, she sighed lustily. "Want dessert?"

"Damn right."

"Okay, but don't order the tiramisu, because then I'd be forced to beg you for a bite, then two, then I'd end up stealing half of it and go into a coma."

Keeping his eyes on hers, he signaled for the waitress with the casual authority of a man used to giving orders. It made Cybil's brow crease.

"Tiramisu," he told the waitress. "Two forks," and made Cybil weak with laughter. "I want to see if putting you into a coma actually shuts you up."

"Won't." She patted her chest as the last laugh bubbled out. "I even talk in my sleep. My sister used to threaten to put a pillow over my head."

"I think I'd like your sister."

"Adria's gorgeous—probably just your type, too. Cool and sophisticated and brilliant. She runs an art gallery in Portsmith."

Preston decided they might as well finish off the wine. It was a very nice Chianti, he mused, which probably explained why he was feeling more relaxed than he had in weeks. Months, he corrected. Maybe years. "So, are you going to fix me up with her?"

"She might go for you," Cybil considered, eyeing him over her glass and enjoying the happy little buzz the wine had given her. "You're great-looking in a sort of rough, I-don't-give-a-damn way. You play a musical instrument, which would appeal to her love and appreciation of the arts. And you're too nasty to treat her like royalty. Too many men do."

"Do they?" he murmured, realizing that his talkative dinner companion was well on her way to being plowed.

"She's so beautiful. They can't help it. Worse, she's irritated when they're dazzled by the way she looks, so she ends up tossing them back. She'd probably end up breaking your heart," she added, gesturing with her glass. "But it might be good for you."

"I don't have a heart," he said when the waitress brought their dessert. "I thought you'd figured that out."

"Sure you do." With a sigh of surrender,

Cybil picked up her fork, scooped up the first bite and tasted with a long moan of pleasure. "You've just got it wrapped in armor so nobody can bayonet it again. God, isn't this wonderful? Don't let me eat any more than this one bite, okay?"

But he was staring at her, amazed that the little lunatic across the hall had zeroed in on him so accurately, so casually, when those who claimed to love him had never come close.

"Why do you say that?"

"Say what? Didn't I tell you not to let me eat any more of this. Are you a sadist?"

"Never mind." Deciding to let it go, he yanked the plate out of her reach. "Mine," he said simply. And proceeded to eat the rest.

He only had to poke her once with his fork to hold her off.

"Well, I had fun." Cybil tucked her arm through his as they walked back toward their building. "Really. That was so much more entertaining than an evening trying to keep Johnny from sliding his hand up my skirt."

For some reason, the image irritated him,

but Preston merely glanced down. "You're not wearing a skirt."

"I know. I wasn't sure I could get out of the date, and this was my automatic defense system."

The breezy saffron-colored slacks struck him abruptly as more sexy than defensive. "So why don't you just break Johnny's face like you did the mugger's the other night?"

"Because Mrs. Wolinsky adores him, and I'd never be able to tell her that the apple of her eye has hands like an ape."

"I think that's a mixed metaphor, but I get the picture. You're a pushover."

"Am not."

"Are so," he said before he caught himself and fell too deeply into the childish game. "You let your friend Joanie—"

"Jody."

"Right, push her cousin on you, and the old lady downstairs sticks you with her nephew with the fast hands, and God knows how many other friends you have dumping their cast-off relatives in your lap. All because you can't just say butt out."

"They mean well."

"They're meddling with your life. It doesn't matter what they mean."

"Oh, I don't know." She blew out a breath and smiled at a young couple strolling on the opposite side of the street. "Take my grandfather. Well, he's not really my grandfather if you get picky, which we don't. He's my dad's sister Shelby's father-in-law. And on my mother's side, she's cousin to the spouses of his other two children. It's a little complicated, if you get picky."

"Which you don't."

"Exactly. There's all this convoluted family connection between Daniel and Anna MacGregor and my parents, so why niggle? My aunt Shelby married their son Alan MacGregor—you might have heard of him. He used to live in the White House."

"The name rings a distant bell."

"And my mother, the former Genviève Grandeau, is a cousin of Justin and Diana Blade—siblings—who married, respectively, Daniel and Anna's other two children, Serena and Caine MacGregor. So Daniel and Anna are Grandpa and Grandma. Is that clear?"

"Yes, I can follow that, but I've forgotten the entire point of the exercise."

"Me, too." She laughed in delight, then had to tighten her grip before she overbalanced. "A little too much wine," she explained. "Anyway, let me think... Yes, I have it. Meddling. We were talking about meddling, which my grand-father—who would be Daniel MacGregor—is the uncontested world champ at. When it comes to matchmaking, he knows no peer. I'm telling you, McQuinn, the man is a wizard. I have..."

She had to stop, use her fingers to count. "Um, I think it's seven cousins so far he's man-aged to match up, marry off. He's terrifying."

"What do you mean 'match up'?"

"He just sort of finds the right person for them—don't ask me how—then he works out a way to put them together, let nature take its course, and before you know it, you've got wed-ding bells and bassinets. He just told me my cousin Ian and his wife are expecting their first. They were married last fall. The man's batting a thousand."

"Does anyone tell him to butt out?"

"Oh, constantly." She tipped up her head and

grinned. "He just doesn't pay attention. I figure he's going to work on Adria or Mel next—give my brother, Matthew, time to season."

"What about you?"

"Oh, I'm too slick for him. I know his canny tricks, and I'm not going to fall in love for years. What about you? Ever been there?"

"Where would that be?"

"Love, McQuinn, don't be dense."

"It's not a place—it's a situation. And there's nothing there."

"Oh, I think there will be," she said dreamily. "Eventually."

For the second time, she pulled up short. "Oh, damn. That's Johnny's car. He's come in from New Jersey after all. Damn, damn, damn. Okay, here's the plan."

She whirled around, shook her head clear when it spun. "I should never have had that last glass of wine, but I'm still master of my fate."

"You bet you are, kid."

"Enough to know you call me 'kid' so you can feel superior and aloof, but that's beside the point. We're just going to stroll on down a few more feet until we're right in front of her window. Very natural, okay?"

"That's a tough one, but I'll see what I can do."

"I just love that nasty streak of sarcasm. Okay, this is fine, this is good. Now, we're going to stand right here, because she's watching, I promise. Any minute you'll see her curtains twitch. Look for it."

Because it seemed harmless, and he was starting to enjoy the way she held on to him, he flicked a glance over her head. "Right on cue. So?"

"You're going to have to kiss me."

His gaze shot back to hers. "Am I?"

"And you're going to have to make it look good. If you do it right, she'll figure Johnny's a lost cause—for a while, anyway. And I'll give you another fifty."

He ran his tongue around his teeth. She had her face tipped back and looked as appealing as a single rosebud in a garden of thorns. "You're going to pay me fifty bucks to kiss you."

"Like a bonus. This could send Johnny back to Jersey for good. Just think of it as being onstage. Doesn't have to mean anything. Is she still watching?"

"Yeah." But he wasn't looking at the window now, and didn't have a clue.

"Great. Good. Make it count, okay. Romantic. Just slide your arms around me, then lean down and—"

"I know how to kiss a woman, Cybil."

"Of course you do. No offense meant whatsoever. But this should be choreographed so that—"

He decided the only way to shut her up was to get on with it, and to get on with it his way. He didn't slide his arms around her—he yanked her against him, and nearly off her feet. He had one glimpse of those big green eyes widening in shock, before his mouth crushed down on hers and sent the next babbling words sliding down her throat.

He was right. That was her last dizzy thought. He was absolutely right. He did know how to kiss a woman.

She had to grab on to his shoulders. Had to rise up to her toes.

She had to moan.

Her head was spinning in fast, giddy circles. Her heart had flipped straight into her throat to block any chance of air. It made her feel helpless, lost, shaky as his mouth pumped heat like a furnace into her body.

And his mouth was so hard, so hard, and stunningly hungry. What else could she do but let him feed?

It was like the dream, he thought. Only better. Much, much better. Her taste hadn't been so unique in his imagination. Her body hadn't trembled with quick, hard little shock waves. Her hands hadn't clawed their way up into his hair to fist while she moaned pure pleasure into his mouth.

He yanked her back, but only to see if her eyes had gone dark, if heat had climbed into her cheeks the way he felt it climb through his system. She only stared at him, her breath coming short and fast through parted lips, her hands still clutched in his hair.

"Next one's on me," he murmured, and took her under again.

A horn blasted. Someone cursed. There was a rush of displaced air from a passing car.

Someone shoved an apartment window open and let out a stream of blistering rock music and the acrid smell of burned dinner.

She might have been on a deserted island with crystal-blue waves crashing at her feet.

When he drew her away the second time, he did so slowly, with his hands skimming down from her shoulders to her elbows, then back in a gesture that stopped only a hint short of a caress. It gave her enough time to feel her head revolve once, like a slow-motion merry-go-round, before it settled weakly on her shoulders.

He wanted to lap her up on the spot, every inch of that flushed, lovely skin. To devour her innate—and, to him, misplaced—cheerfulness that shone out of her like sunlight. He wanted all that impossible, unflagging energy under him, over him, open to him.

And he had no doubt that once he had, he'd leave them both bitter.

Now the hands that lingered on her shoulders eased her back off her toes. Steadied her. Released her. "I think that ought to do it."

"Do it?" she echoed, staring up at him.

"Satisfy Mrs. Wolinsky."

The Perfect Neighbour

"Mrs. Wolinsky?" Absolutely blank, she shook her head. "Oh. Oh, yeah." She blew out a long breath and decided her system might settle sometime before the end of the next decade. "If it doesn't it's hopeless. You're awfully good at it, McQuinn."

A reluctant smile flitted around his mouth. The woman was damn near irresistible, he thought, and, taking her arm, turned her toward the front of the building. "You're not half-bad at it yourself, kid."

Chapter 4

Cybil sang as she worked, belting out a duet with Aretha Franklin. Behind her, the open window welcomed the cool April breeze and the amazing noise that was the downtown streets in brilliant sunshine.

The stream of light was no sunnier than her mood.

Turning to the mirror on the wall beside her, she tried to work her face into a state of shock to help her with a character expression. But all she could do was grin.

She'd been kissed before. She'd been held

by and against a man before. As far as she was concerned comparing all her other experiences to that stunning sidewalk embrace with the man across the hall was like pitting a firecracker against a nuclear attack.

One hissed, popped and was momentarily entertaining. The other detonated and changed the landscape for centuries.

It had left her marvelously dizzy for hours.

She loved the sensation, adored every moment of that giddy, slack-muscled, purely feminine rush. Could there be anything more wonderful than feeling weak and strong, foolish and wise, confused and aware all at the same time?

And all she had to do was close her eyes, let her mind wander back, to feel it all over again.

She wondered what he was thinking, what he was feeling. No one could be unaffected by an experience of that…magnitude. And after all, he'd been right there with her at ground zero. A man couldn't kiss a woman like that and not suffer some potent residual effects.

Suffering, Cybil decided, as her body tingled, was highly underrated.

She chuckled; she sighed; then, bending over her work, sang with Aretha about the joys of feeling like a natural woman.

"God, Cyb, it's freezing in here!"

Cybil looked up, beamed. "Hi, Jody. Hi, sweet Charlie."

The baby gave her a sleepy-eyed smile as Jody strode to the window with him cocked on her hip. "You're sitting in front of an open window. It can't be more than sixty degrees out there." With a little grunt, Jody shoved the window closed.

"I was feeling kind of warm." Cybil set her pencil aside to stroke Charlie's pudgy cheek. "It's miraculous, isn't it, that men start out this way? As pretty little babies? Then they…wow, boy do they grow up into something else."

"Yeah." Puzzled, Jody frowned, examined her friend's somewhat glassy eyes. "You look funny. Are you okay?" Jody laid a maternal hand on Cybil's forehead. "No fever. Stick out your tongue."

Cybil obeyed, crossing her eyes as she did and making Charlie bubble with laughter. "I'm not sick. I'm fabulous. I feel like a million after taxes."

"Hmm." Unconvinced, Jody pursed her lips. "I'm going to put Charlie down for his morning nap. He's zonked. Then I'll get us some coffee and you can tell me what's going on."

"Sure. Um-hmm." Dreaming again, Cybil picked up a red pen and began to doodle pretty little hearts on scrap paper.

Since that was fun, she drew larger ones, sketching Preston's face inside one.

He had a great one, she mused. Hard mouth, cool eyes, very strong features set off by that thick, dark hair. But that mouth softened a bit when he smiled. And his eyes weren't cool when he laughed.

She loved making him laugh. He always sounded just a little out of practice. She could help him with that, she mused, drawing his face again with the warmth of laughter added. After all, one of her nice little talents was making people laugh.

And after she'd helped him find some steady work, he wouldn't have so much to worry about.

She'd get him some work, make certain that he ate regular meals—she was always cooking too much for one person anyway—and she was sure she could find someone who had a second-hand sofa they were willing to part with on the cheap.

She knew enough people to start the ball rolling here and there for him. He'd feel better, wouldn't he, once he was more settled in, more secure? It wouldn't be like meddling. That was her grandfather's territory. She would just be helping out a neighbor.

A gorgeous, sexy neighbor who could kiss a woman straight into the paradisc of delirium.

Of course that wouldn't be why she was doing it. Cybil shook herself, turned the scraps of paper over a little guiltily. She'd helped Mr. Peebles find a good podiatrist, hadn't she? And nobody would consider him a cool-eyed Adonis with great hands, would they?

Of course not.

She was just being a good neighbor. And if there were any other...benefits, well, so what?

Satisfied with her plans, she folded her legs under her and got back to work.

* * *

Jody settled the baby, thinking as she always did when she tucked him in that he was the most beautiful child ever to grace the planet. When his heavy eyes shut, his blanket was smoothed and his favorite teddy bear left on guard, she trotted downstairs to turn down the music.

As at home in Cybil's kitchen as her own, she poured morning coffee into two thick yellow mugs, sniffed out a couple of cranberry muffins, then loaded up a tray.

The midmorning ritual was one of her favorite parts of the day.

In the past few years, Cybil had become as close as a sister to her. Closer, Jody thought, wrinkling her nose. Her own sisters were always bragging about their husbands, their kids, their houses—when anyone could see her Chuck and her Charlie were miles superior. But Cybil listened. Cybil had held her hand through the difficult decision to quit her job and stay home with the baby full-time. It had been Cybil who'd stood by during those early days when she and Chuck had been panicked over every burp and sniffle Charlie had made.

There was no better friend in the world. Which was why Jody was determined to see Cybil blissfully happy.

She carried the tray up, set it on the table, then handed Cybil her mug.

"Thanks, Jody."

"Great strip this morning. I can't believe Emily decking herself out in a trench coat and fedora and tailing Mr. Mysterious all over Soho. Where does she get this stuff?"

"She's a creature of impulse and drama." Cybil broke off a piece of a muffin. It was usual for them to discuss Emily and the other characters as separate people. "And she's nosy. She just has to know."

"What about you? Did you find out anything yet about our Mr. Mysterious?"

"Yeah." Cybil said it on a sigh. "His name's McQuinn."

"I heard that." Instantly alert, Jody jabbed out a finger. "You sighed."

"No, I was just breathing."

"Uh-uh, you sighed. What gives?"

"Well, actually…" She was dying to talk about it. "We sort of went out last night."

"Went out? Like a date?" Quickly, Jody pulled over a chair, sat, leaned close. "Where, how, when? Details, Cyb."

"Okay. So." Cybil swiveled so they were face to face. "You know how Mrs. Wolinsky's always trying to fix me up with her nephew?"

"Not again?" Jody rolled her dark eyes. "Why can't she see you two are totally wrong for each other?"

Vast affection prevented Cybil from mentioning that it might be the same selective blindness that prevented Jody from seeing the flaws in the Cybil-Frank match.

"She just loves him. But anyway, she'd cooked up another date for me for last night, and I just couldn't face it. You have to swear you won't tell her—or anyone."

"Except Chuck."

"Husbands are excluded from the vow of silence in this case. I told her I already had a date—with McQuinn."

"You had a date with 3B?"

"No, I just told her I did because I was flustered. You know how I start babbling when I lie."

"You should practice." Nodding, Jody bit into a muffin. "You'd get better at it."

"Maybe. So after I tell her, I realize she's going to be looking for us to leave together, and I have to cut some kind of deal with McQuinn to go along with it. I gave him a hundred and bought him dinner."

"You paid him." Jody's eyes widened, then narrowed in speculation. "That's brilliant. The whole time I was dating—especially during that drought period I told you about my sophomore year in college? I never thought about just offering a guy some money to have dinner with me. How'd you settle on the hundred? Do you think that's, like, the going rate?"

"It seemed right. He's not working regularly, you know. And I figured he could use the money and a hot meal. We had a good time," she added with a new smile. "Really good. Just spaghetti and conversation. Well, mostly one-sided conversation, as McQuinn doesn't say a lot."

"McQuinn." Jody let the name roll over her tongue. "Still sounds mysterious. You don't know his first name."

"It never came up. Anyway, it gets better. We're walking back. I think I loosened him up, Jody. He really seemed relaxed, almost friendly. Then I see Johnny Wolinsky's car, and I panicked. I'm figuring she's not going to stop trying to shove him at me unless she thinks I've got a guy. So I cut another deal with McQuinn and offered him fifty bucks to kiss me."

Jody pursed her lips, then sipped coffee. "I think you should've said that was included in the hundred."

"No, we'd already defined terms, and there wasn't time to renegotiate. She was looking out the window. So he did, right there on the sidewalk."

"Wow." Jody grabbed the rest of her muffin. "What move did he use?"

"He just sort of *yanked* me against him."

"Oh, man. The yank. I really like the yank."

"Then I was plastered there, up on my toes because he's tall."

"Yeah." Jody chewed, licked crumbs off her lips. "He's tall. And built."

"Really built, Jody. I mean the man is like a rock."

"Oh, God." On the moan, Jody rubbed her stomach. "Wow. Okay, so you're plastered up there, on your toes. What next?"

"Then he just…swooped."

"Oh-oh, the yank and swoop." Crumbs scattered as Jody waved her hands. "It's a classic. Hardly any guy can really pull it off, though. Chuck did on date six. That's how we ended up back at my apartment, eating Chinese in bed."

"McQuinn pulled it off. He really, really pulled it off. Then, while my head was exploding, he yanked me back, just looked at me."

"Man. Man."

"Then he just…did it all again."

"A double." Near tears with vicarious excitement, Jody gripped Cybil's hand. "You got a double. There are women who go all their lives without a double. Dreaming of, yes, but never achieving the double yank and swoop."

"It was my first," Cybil confessed. "It… was…*great!*"

"Okay, okay, just the kiss part, okay? Just the lips and tongues and teeth thing. How was that?"

"It was very hot."

"Oh…I'm going to have to open the window. I'm starting to sweat."

She jumped up, shoved up the window and took a deep gulp of air. "So, it was hot. Very hot. Keep going."

"It was like being, well, devoured. When your system just goes…" At a loss, she lifted her hands, wiggled them wildly. "And your head's circling around about a foot above your shoulders, and…I don't know how to describe it."

"You've got to." Desperate, Jody squeezed Cybil's shoulders. "I'm on the edge here. Try this—on the one-to-ten scale, where did it hit?"

Cybil closed her eyes. "There is no scale."

"There's always a scale—you can say off the scale, but there's always a scale."

"No, Jody, there is no scale."

Eyeing Cybil, Jody stepped back. "The no scale is an urban myth."

"It exists," Cybil said soberly. "The no scale exists, my friend, and has now been documented."

"Sweet Lord. I have to sit down." She did

so, her eyes never leaving Cybil's face. "You experienced a no scale. I believe you, Cyb. Thousands wouldn't. Millions would scoff, but I believe you."

"I knew I could count on you."

"You know what this means, don't you? He's ruined you for anything less. Even a ten won't satisfy you now. You'll always be looking for the next no scale."

"I've thought of that." Considering, Cybil picked up her pencil to tap. "I believe it's possible to live a full and happy life, hitting with some regularity between seven and ten, even after this experience. Man goes to the moon, Jody. Travels through space and time, finds himself on another world, but only briefly. He must come back to earth and live."

"That's so wise," Jody murmured, and had to dig a tissue out of her pocket. "So brave."

"Thank you. But in the meantime," Cybil added with a grin, "there's no harm in knocking on the door across the hall from time to time."

Because she didn't want to appear overanxious, Cybil put in a full morning's work. She didn't break until after two, when she thought her neighbor might enjoy sharing a cup of coffee, maybe a nice walk in the April sunshine.

He really had to get out of that apartment more, she decided. Take advantage of all the city had to offer. She imagined him brooding behind his locked door, worried about his lack of employment, the bills.

She was certain she could help him with that. There was no reason she couldn't put a buzz in a few ears and get him a few gigs to tide him over.

She heard the sax begin to weep as she stood in her bedroom fussing with her makeup. It made her tingle again, the low, sexy throb of it.

He deserved a break, something to take that cynical gleam out of his eyes. Something that would prove to him life was full of surprises. She wanted to help him. There was a quality about him—an underlying unhappiness she was driven to smooth away.

After all, she'd made him laugh. She'd helped him relax. If she could do it once, she could do it again. She badly wanted to see him laugh again, to hear that sardonic edge to his voice when he made some pithy comment, to see that grin flash when she said or did something that got through his cynical shield.

And if they lit a few sexual sparks between them while she was at it, what was wrong with that?

She was on her way downstairs, and singing again, when the buzzer from the entrance door sounded on her intercom.

"Yes?"

"I'm looking for McQuinn. 3A?"

"No, he's 3B."

"Well, damn it. Why doesn't he answer?"

"Oh, he probably doesn't hear you. He's practicing."

"Buzz me in, will you, sweetie? I'm his agent and I'm running way behind."

"His agent." Cybil perked up. If he had an agent, Cybil wanted to meet her. She'd already thought of half a dozen names to pass on for possible jobs. "Sure. Come on up."

She released the door, then opened her own and waited.

The woman who stepped out of the little-used elevator looked very professional, very successful, Cybil noted with some surprise, in her snazzy power suit of drop-dead red. She was thin and wiry, with a sharp-featured face, dark-blue eyes that were snapping with annoyance and an incredibly fabulous mane of streaked blond hair.

She moved with the precision of a bullet and carried a leather briefcase that Cybil estimated cost the equivalent of a month's rent on a good uptown apartment.

So, she mused, why was her client scrambling for work if his agent could afford designer duds and pricey accessories?

"3A?"

"Yes, I'm Cybil."

"Amanda Dresher. Thanks, Cybil. Our boy here isn't answering his phone, and apparently forgot we had a one o'clock at the Four Seasons."

"The Four Seasons?" Baffled, Cybil stared. "On Park?"

"Is there another?" With a laugh, Mandy pressed the buzzer on 3B and—knowing her prey—held it down. "Our Preston's loaded with talent, but he's my biggest pain in the butt."

"Preston." It only took a minute for the confusion to form, settle, then clear away. "Preston McQuinn." She let out a shaky breath that was equal parts betrayal and mortification. *"A Tangle of Souls."*

"That's our boy," Mandy said cheerfully. "Come on, come on, McQuinn, answer the damn door. I thought when he decided to stay in the city for a couple months I'd be able to keep better track of him. But it's still an obstacle course. Ah, here we go."

They both heard the bad-tempered snick of locks being turned. Then he yanked open the door. "What the hell do you...Mandy?"

"You missed lunch," she snapped. "You're not answering the phone."

"I forgot lunch. The phone didn't ring."

"Did you charge the battery?"

"Probably not." He stood where he was, staring across the hall to where Cybil watched him with wounded eyes in a pale face. "Come on in. Just give me a minute."

"I've already given you an hour." She tossed

a glance over her shoulder as she walked inside. "Thanks for buzzing me up, sweetie."

"No problem. No problem at all." Then Cybil looked Preston dead in the eye. "You bastard," she said quietly, and closed her door.

"Don't you have any place to sit in here?" Mandy complained behind him.

"No. Yes. Upstairs. Damn it," he muttered, despising the slide of guilt. Doing his best to shrug it off, he closed his door. "I don't use the space down here much."

"No kidding. So who's the kid across the hall?" she asked as she set her briefcase on the kitchen counter.

"Nobody. Campbell, Cybil Campbell."

"I thought she looked familiar. 'Friends and Neighbors.' I know her agent. He's crazy about her. Claims she's the only ego-proof, neurosis-free client he's ever had. Never whines, doesn't miss deadlines, never demands coddling, and is currently making him a fat pile of money on the sales of her trade books and calendars, plus the merchandising tie-ins."

She sent Preston a baleful look. "I wonder what it's like to have a neurosis-free client who remembers lunch dates and sends me gifts on my birthday."

"The neuroses are part of the package, but I'm sorry about lunch."

Annoyance faded into concern. "What's up, Preston? You look ragged out. Is the play stalled?"

"No, it's moving. Better than I expected. I just didn't get a lot of sleep."

"Out playing your horn till all hours again?"

"No." Thinking of the woman in 3A, he thought. Pacing the floor. Wanting the woman in 3A. The woman who now, undoubtedly, considered him a slightly lower life-form than slime.

"Just a bad night, Mandy."

"Okay." Because as irritated as he could make her, she cared about him. She crossed the room to give his tensed shoulders a brisk rub. "But you owe me lunch. How about some coffee?"

"There's some on the stove. It was fresh at six this morning."

"Let's start over, then. I'll make it." She

moved behind the counter. After she had the coffee going, she poked into the cupboards. She considered Preston's welfare part of her job.

"God, McQuinn, are you on a hunger strike? There's nothing in here but potato-chip crumbs and what once might have been cracked-wheat bread and is now a science project."

"I didn't make it to the market yesterday." Again his gaze flicked to the door and his mind to Cybil. "Mostly I call in dinner."

"On the phone you don't answer?"

"I'll recharge the battery, Mandy."

"See that you do. If you'd remembered sooner, we'd be sitting in the Four Seasons right now, drinking Cristal to celebrate." She grinned as she leaned on the counter toward him. "I closed the deal, Preston. *A Tangle of Souls* is going to be a major motion picture. You got the producers you wanted, the director you wanted and the option to do the screenplay yourself. All that plus a tidy little fee."

She gave him an amount in seven figures.

"I don't want them to screw it up," was Preston's first reaction.

"Leave it to you." Mandy sighed. "If there's a downside, you find it. So do the screenplay."

"No." He shook his head, walking to the window to try to absorb the news. A film would change the intimacy the play had achieved in the theater. But it would also take his work to millions. And the work mattered to him.

"I don't want to go back there, Mandy. Not that deep."

She poured two cups of coffee and joined him at the window. "Supervisory capacity. Consultant?"

"Yeah, that works for me. Fix it, will you?"

"I can do that. Now, if you'll stop turning cartwheels and dancing on the ceiling, we can talk about your work in progress."

Her dry tone got through, made his lips twitch. He set his coffee on the windowsill, turned and took her sharp-boned face in his hands. "You're the best, and certainly the most patient agent in the business."

"You're so right. I hope you're as proud of yourself as I am. Are you going to call your family?"

"Let me sit on it a couple days."

"It's going to hit the trades, Preston. You don't want them to hear about it that way."

"No, you're right. I'll call them." Finally, he smiled. "After I charge the phone. Why don't I clean up and take you out for that champagne."

"Why don't you. Oh, one more thing," she added as he started for the stairs. "Pretty Miss 3A? Are you going to tell me what's going on between you?"

"I'm not sure there's anything to tell," he murmured.

He still wasn't sure when he knocked on her door later that evening. But he knew he had to answer for that look he'd put in her eyes.

Not that it had been any of her business in the first place, he reminded himself. He hadn't asked her to come nosing around. In fact he'd done everything to discourage her.

Until last night, he thought, and hissed out a breath.

Bad judgment, he decided. It had just been bad judgment. He shouldn't have followed impulse and gone along with her. Shouldn't have compounded the mistake by enjoying himself.

Or by kissing her.

Which he wouldn't have done, his mind circled back, if she hadn't asked him to.

When she pulled open the door, he was ready with an apology. "Look, I'm sorry," he began, delivering it with an impatient edge of annoyance. "But it was none of your business anyway. Let's just straighten this out."

He started to step in, coming up short when she slapped a hand on his chest.

"I don't want you in here."

"For God's sake. You started it. Maybe I let it get out of hand, but—"

"Started what?"

"This," he snapped, furious at the sudden lack of words, hating the kicked-puppy look in her eyes.

"All right, I started it. I should never have brought you cookies. That was devious of me. I shouldn't have worried that you didn't have a job, shouldn't have bought you a decent meal because I thought you couldn't afford it on your own."

"Damn it, Cybil."

"You let me think that. You let me believe

you were some poor, out-of-work musician, and I'm sure you had a few private laughs over it. The brilliant, award-winning playwright Preston McQuinn, author of the stunning, emotionally wrenching *A Tangle of Souls*. But I bet you're surprised I even know your work. A bubblehead like me."

She shoved him back a step. "What would a fluffy comic-strip writer know about real art, after all? About serious theater, about *literature?* Why shouldn't you have a few laughs at my expense? You narrow-minded, arrogant creep." Her voice broke when she'd promised herself she wouldn't let it. "I was only trying to help you."

"I didn't ask for your help. I didn't want it." He could see she was close to tears. The closer she got, the more furious he became. He knew how women used tears to destroy a man. He wouldn't let it happen. "My work's my own business."

"Your work's produced on Broadway. That makes it public business," she shot back. "And that has nothing to do with pretending to be a sax player."

"I play the damn sax because I like to play the damn sax. I didn't pretend to be anything. You assumed."

"You let me assume."

"What if I did? I moved in here for a little peace and quiet. To be left alone. The next thing I know you're bringing me cookies, then you're following me and I'm spending half the night in the police station. Then you're asking me to go out so you can slip by a seventy-year-old woman because you don't have the guts to tell her to butt out of your personal life. And you top it off by offering me fifty dollars to kiss you."

Humiliation had the first tear spilling over, trailing slowly down her cheek and making his stomach clench. "Don't." The order whipped out of him. "Don't start that."

"Don't cry when you humiliate me? When you make me feel stupid and ridiculous and ashamed?" She didn't bother to dash the tears away but simply looked at him out of unapologetically drenched eyes. "Sorry, I don't work that way. I cry when someone hurts me."

"You brought it on yourself." He had to say

it, was desperate to believe it. And escaped by stalking to his own door.

"You have the facts, Preston," she said quietly. "You have them all in an accurate row. But you've missed the feelings behind them. I brought you cookies because I thought you could use a friend. I've already apologized for following you, but I'll apologize again."

"I don't want—"

"I'm not finished," she said with such quiet dignity he felt one more wave of guilt. "I took you to dinner because I didn't want to hurt a very nice woman, and I thought you might be hungry. I enjoyed being with you, and I felt something when you kissed me. I thought you did, too. So you're right." She nodded coolly, even as another tear slid down her cheek. "I did bring it all on myself. I suppose you save all your emotions for your work, and can't find the way to let them into your life. I'm sorry for you. And I'm sorry I trod on your sacred ground. I won't do it again."

Before he could think of how to respond, she shut her door. He heard her locks slide into place with quick, deliberate clicks. Turning, he let himself in to his own apartment, followed her example by closing, then locking, the door behind him.

He had what he wanted, he told himself. Solitude. Quiet. She wouldn't come knocking on his door again to interrupt his thoughts, to distract him, to tangle him up in feelings and conversations he didn't want. In feelings he didn't know what to do with.

And he stood, exhausted by the storm and sick of himself, staring at an empty room.

Chapter 5

He couldn't sleep, except in patches. And the patches were riddled with dreams. In them he would find himself wrapped around Cybil. His back in a corner, up against a wall, at the edge of a cliff.

It always seemed as if she'd maneuvered him there, where there was nowhere to go but to her.

And when he did, the dreams became brutally erotic, so that when he managed to rip himself from them, he found himself aroused, furious and filled with the memory, the taste, of her in his mouth.

He couldn't eat, found himself picking at food when he bothered with it at all. Nothing satisfied him; everything reminded him of that simple meal they'd shared a few nights before.

He lived on coffee until his nerves jangled and his stomach burned in protest.

But he could work. It seemed he could always flow into a story, into his people, when his emotions were pumped. It was painful to tear those feelings out of his own heart and have the characters he created gobble them greedily up. But he relished the exchange, even fed on it.

He remembered what Cybil had said before she'd closed the door on him—that he used all his emotions in his work and didn't know how to let them into his life.

She was right, and it was better that way. There were, to his mind, very few people he could trust with feelings. His parents, his sister—though his need to fulfill their expectations of and for him was a double-edged sword.

Then Delta and André, those rare friends he allowed himself and who expected no more from him than what he wanted himself.

Mandy, who pushed him when he needed

pushing, listened when he needed to unburden and somehow managed to care about him even when he didn't.

He didn't want a woman digging her way into his heart. Not again. He'd learned his lesson there, and had kept any and all applicants since Pamela out of that vulnerable territory.

She'd cured him, he thought, with lies, deceptions, betrayals. A man could learn a good deal at the tender age of twenty-five that held him in good stead for the duration. Since he'd stopped believing in love, he never wasted time looking for it.

But he couldn't stop thinking of Cybil.

He'd heard her go out several times in the last three days. He'd been distracted more than once by the laughter and voices and music from her apartment.

She wasn't suffering, he reminded himself. So why was he?

It was guilt, he decided. He'd hurt her and it had been neither necessary nor intentional. He'd been charmed by her; reluctantly, but charmed nonetheless. He hadn't meant to make her feel foolish, to bruise her feelings. Tears could still rip at him, even knowing how false and sly they could be when they slid down a woman's cheek.

But they hadn't looked false or sly on Cybil, he remembered. They'd looked as natural as rain.

He wasn't going to resolve the problem—his problem, he thought—until he'd settled with her. He hadn't apologized well; he could admit that. So he'd apologize again now that she'd had some time to get those emotions of hers she was so free with under some control.

There was no reason for them to be enemies, after all. She was the granddaughter of a man he admired and respected. He doubted Daniel MacGregor would return the compliment if he learned that Preston McQuinn had made his little girl cry.

And, Preston realized, Daniel MacGregor's opinion mattered to him.

So, a little voice nagged at him, did Cybil's.

That was why he was pacing the living area of his apartment instead of working. He'd heard her go out, again, but hadn't been quite quick enough to get downstairs and into the hall before she'd gone.

He could wait her out, Preston thought. She had to come back sometime. And when she did, he'd head her off and offer her a very civilized apology. It was blatantly obvious the woman had a soft heart. She'd have to forgive him. Once she had, they could go back to being neighbors.

There was the matter of the hundred dollars, as well, which instead of amusing him as it had initially, now made him feel nasty.

He was sure she'd be ready to laugh the whole thing off now. How long could that kind of cheerful nature hold a grudge?

He would have been surprised to find out just how long, and how well, if he'd seen Cybil's face as she rode the elevator up to the third floor.

It annoyed her, outrageously, that she had to pass the man's door to get to her own. It infuriated her that doing so made her think of him, remember how stupid she'd been—and how much more stupid he'd made her feel.

She shifted the weight of the two bags of

groceries she carried in either arm and tried to dig out her key so she wouldn't have to linger in the hallway a second longer than necessary.

The elevator gave its usual announcing thud when it reached her floor. She was still searching for the elusive key when she stepped off.

Her teeth set when she saw him, and her eyes went frosty.

"Cybil." He'd never seen her eyes cold, and the chill of them threw him off rhythm. "Ah, let me give you a hand with those."

"I don't need a hand, thank you." She could only pray to grow a third one, rapidly, that could find her bloody keys.

"Yes, you do, if you're going to keep rooting around in that purse."

He tried a smile, then scowled as they played tug-of-war with one of her bags. In the end he just wrenched it out of her grip. "Look, damn it, I said I was sorry. How many times do I have to say it before you get out of this snit you're in?"

"Go to hell," she shot back. "How many times do I have to say it before you start to feel the heat?"

She finally snagged the key, jabbed it into the lock. "Give me my groceries."

"I'll take them in for you."

"I said give me the damn bag." They were back to tugging, until she hissed out a breath. "Keep them, then."

She shoved open the door, but before she could slam it in his face, he'd shoved it open again and pushed his way inside. Their eyes met, both narrowed, and he thought he caught a glint of violence in hers.

"Don't even think about it," he warned her. "I'm not an underweight mugger."

She thought she could still do some damage but decided it would only make him seem more important than she'd determined he would be. Instead, she turned on the heel of her pink suede sneakers, dumped her bag on the counter. When he did the same, she nodded briskly.

"Thanks. Now you've delivered them. Want a tip?"

"Very funny. Let's just settle this first." He reached in his pocket, where he'd folded the hundred-dollar bill she'd given him. "Here."

She flicked the money a disinterested glance. "I'm not taking it back. You earned it."

"I'm not keeping your money over what turned out to be a bad joke."

"Bad joke!" The ice in her eyes turned to sharp green flames. "Is that what it was? Well, ha-ha. Now that you bring it up, I owe you another fifty, don't I?"

That hit the mark, had his jaw clenching as she grabbed up her purse. "Don't push it, Cybil. Take the money back."

"No."

"I said take the damn money." He grabbed her wrist, yanked her around and crumpled the bill into her palm. "Now…" Then watched in astonishment as she ripped a hundred dollars into confetti.

"There, problem solved."

"That," he said on what he hoped was a calming breath, "was amazingly stupid."

"Stupid? Well, why break pattern? You can go now," she said.

Her voice was so suddenly regal, so completely princess to peon, he nearly blinked. "Very good, very effective," he murmured.

"The lady-of-the-manor tone was so utterly unexpected."

Her next suggestion, delivered in the same haughty tone, was also utterly unexpected, to the point, and made him blink.

"That works, too," he acknowledged. "And I don't think you meant that in a romantic sense."

She simply turned, stalked around the counter and began to put away her groceries. If insults and swearing didn't work, perhaps ignoring him would.

It might have if he hadn't seen her fingers tremble as she pushed a box into the cupboard. And seeing it, he felt everything inside him fade but the guilt.

"Cybil, I'm sorry." He watched her hand hesitate, then grab a soup can and shove it away. "It took on a life of its own, and I didn't do anything to stop it. I should have."

"You didn't have to lie to me. I'd have left you alone."

"I didn't lie—or didn't start out to. But I let you assume something other than the truth. I want my privacy. I need it."

"You've got it. I'm not the one who just bullied his way into someone's apartment."

"No, you're not." He stuck his hands in his pockets, dragged them out again and laid them on the counter. "I hurt you, and I didn't have to. I'm sorry for it."

She closed her eyes as she felt the gate she'd sworn to keep locked on her heart creak open. "Why did you?"

"Because I thought it would keep you on your own side of the hall. Because you were a little too appealing for comfort. And because part of me got a kick out of you wanting to help me find work."

He saw her shoulders draw up at that and winced. "I didn't mean it that way. Cybil, how could I not be amused when you offered me a hundred dollars to have dinner with you? A hundred dollars so you could spare an old woman's feelings and get some out-of-work sax player a hot meal. It was…sweet. That's not a word that comes easy to me."

"It's humiliating," she muttered, and grabbed the second bag and began shoving produce into the fridge.

"Don't let it be." He took a chance and walked around the counter so they both stood in the kitchen. "It only backfired because the timing was off, and that's my fault. If I'd told you who I was over dinner, as I should have, you'd have laughed about it. Instead, I made you cry, and I can't stand knowing that."

She stood where she was, staring into the refrigerator. She hadn't expected him to care, for it to matter to him. But it did. She simply couldn't hold out against a caring heart.

Drawing a deep breath, she told herself they would start fresh. Try for casual friends. "Want a beer?"

Every knot in his shoulders loosened. "Oh, yeah."

"Figured." She reached in for a bottle, disposed of the top, reached for a glass. "I haven't heard you talk so much at one time since I met you." When she turned, offering the beer, her eyes were smiling. "You must be dry."

"Thanks."

Her dimple fluttered. "But I'm out of cookies."

"You could always make some more."

"Maybe." She turned away to deal with the groceries. "But I was thinking about baking a pie." Tossing a look over her shoulder, she lifted a brow. "We never did have that pie."

"No, we didn't."

Too appealing for comfort, he thought again. She was wearing an oversize cotton shirt, plain white. Leggings the color of summer skies, those silly shoes.

Since she'd been marketing, he doubted that the just-under-the-smoldering-point perfume had been dabbed on to please anyone but herself, and had no idea why she would wear two gold hoops in one ear and a single diamond stud in the other.

But it all combined into one fascinating package.

When she turned back to reach into the bag again, he took her wrist with his free hand. "Are we on level ground now?"

"Looks like."

"Then there's something else." He set the beer down. "I dream about you."

Now it was her mouth that went dry. And her

stomach erupted with the crazed flapping of a hundred wings. "What?"

"I dream about you," he repeated, and stepped forward until her back was against the refrigerator. Her back against the wall this time, he thought. Not his. "About being with you, touching you." Watching her face, he skimmed his fingertips over the tops of her breasts. "And I wake up tasting you."

"Oh, God."

"You said you felt something when I kissed you, and thought I did, too." With his eyes still on hers, he ran his hands down her sides to her hips. "You were right."

Weak at the knees, she swallowed. Hard. "I was?"

"Yeah. And I want to feel it again."

She strained back as he leaned forward. "Wait!"

His mouth paused a breath from hers. "Why?"

And her mind went blank. "I don't know."

His lips curved in one of his rare smiles. "Stop me when you do," he suggested, then captured her.

It was the same. She was sure it wouldn't be, couldn't be the same fast, hot spin of heart and mind and body. But all those parts of her seemed to have been waiting, and poised to leap. Jody was right, she thought dimly. He'd ruined her.

Bright, fresh, soft as a sunbeam. She was all those things. Warm, sweet, generous. All the things he'd forgotten to need were trembling in his arms.

And he wanted them, wanted her with a quick punch of greed he hadn't expected.

On an oath, he savaged her throat. "Here. Right here."

"No." It was the last thing she'd expected to hear come out of her own mouth when his hands were making her ache for more. Even as the need roared in her blood she said it again. "No. Wait."

He lifted his head, kept eyes that had gone the color of a storm at sea on hers. "Why?"

"Because I…" Her head fell back on a moan when his hands, slow and firm, stroked up her body, awakening every pore.

"I want you." His thumbs circled her breasts, over them. "You want me."

"Yes, but—" Her hands opened and closed on his shoulders as she fought off a new spurt of longing. "There are a few things I don't let myself do on impulse. I'm really sorry to say this is one of them."

She opened her eyes again, let out one more shaky breath. How closely he watched her, she realized. How sharply, even with desire clouding his mind. He could step back from it, look through it, and measure.

"It's not a game, Preston."

He lifted a brow, surprised that she'd understood his thoughts so clearly. "No? No," he decided, because he believed her. "You wouldn't be good at that kind of game, would you?"

Someone had been, she thought, and was suddenly, brutally sorry for him. "I don't know. I've never played it."

He stepped back, shrugged and seemed completely in control again while her system continued to jangle. Unconsciously, she lifted her fingertips to her throat where his mouth had aroused dozens of raw nerves.

"I need time before I share myself that way. Making love is a gift and shouldn't be given thoughtlessly."

Her words touched him and, for reasons he couldn't understand, settled him. "It often is."

"Not for me." She shook her head. "Not from me."

Because he had a sudden urge to stroke her cheek, he hooked his thumbs in his front pockets. Better not to touch again, he reasoned. Not quite yet. "And telling me that is supposed to make me content to step back?"

"Telling you that is supposed to make you understand why I said no, when I want to say yes. When we both know you could make me say yes."

Heat flicked into his eyes. "That's a dangerous kind of honesty you have there."

"You need the truth." She didn't believe she'd ever known anyone who needed it more. "And I don't lie to men I'm planning to be intimate with."

He stepped forward again, watched her lips tremble on a strangled breath. He could make her say yes...and the power of that was heady.

Using it, he realized, would damage something he wasn't completely sure he believed existed.

"You need time," he said. "You got an estimate on that?"

Her breath shuddered out again. "Right now it feels like five minutes ago. But…" She managed a weak laugh when his lips curved. "I can't really say, except you'll be the first to know."

"Maybe we could shave a couple of days off it," he murmured, and indulged himself by leaning down to rub his lips over hers.

Hoping it would focus her, she kept her eyes open. But her vision went blurry at the edges. "Um, yes, that's probably going to work."

"Let's shoot for a week," he murmured, deepening the kiss degree by degree until she went limp.

When he stepped back, she pressed a hand to her heart. "Fortnight. I've always liked that word, haven't you? We could try for a fortnight."

The last thing he'd expected to do when buffeted by desire was laugh. "I think we'll save that one for later."

"Right, good. Smart." She concentrated on

breathing as he turned and picked up his beer. "Well, I have all this..." She gestured vaguely.

"Food?" he suggested. Delighted by her bewilderment.

"Food, yes. I have all this food. I thought I'd fix some..."

He waited a beat while she pressed her hand to her temple and frowned at the stove. "Dinner?"

"That's it. Ha. Dinner. Funny how words just skip out of reach sometimes. I'm going to fix dinner." She blew out a breath. "Would you like to stay for dinner?"

He sipped his beer, leaned back against the counter. "Can I watch you cook?"

"Sure. You can sit there and maybe slice vegetables or something."

"Okay." Because the idea had amazing appeal, he skirted the counter to sit on a stool. "You cook a lot?"

"Yes, I guess. I really like to cook. It's an adventurous process, all the ingredients, heat, timing, the mix of smells and textures and tastes."

"So...do you ever cook naked?"

She paused in the act of sniffing a glossy red

pepper. Giggling, she set it on the counter between them. "McQuinn, you made a joke." She put a hand over his, squeezed. "I'm so proud."

"No, I didn't. That was a perfectly serious question."

When she laughed, leaned over to grab his face and kiss him noisily on the mouth, he wouldn't have recognized his own foolish grin. "So do you?"

"Never when I'm sautéing chicken. Which is what I'm about to do."

"That's all right. I have an excellent imagination."

She laughed again; then, catching the wicked gleam in his eyes, cleared her throat. "I think I want some wine. Do you want wine?" He only lifted his nearly full glass of beer. "Oh, yeah."

She took a bottle of white out of the refrigerator, then turned back, giggling again. "You're going to have to stop that."

"Stop what?"

"Stop making me think I'm naked. Go put on some music," she ordered, waving a hand toward the living area. "Maybe open a window, because it's really hot in here, and give me a minute to clear the lust out of my head so I can think of something else to talk about."

"You never have trouble talking."

"You consider that an insult," she said as he slid off the stool. "I don't. I'm a conversation connoisseur."

"Is that the current term for chatterbox?"

"Well, you're just full of wit and humor tonight, aren't you?" And nothing could have pleased her more.

"Must be the company," he murmured, then cocked a brow as he flipped through her CDs. "You have decent taste in music."

"You were expecting otherwise?"

"I wasn't expecting Fats Waller, Aretha, B.B. King. Of course, you've got plenty of chirpy stuff in here, too."

"What's wrong with chirpy music?"

In answer, he held up a CD of *The Partridge Family's Greatest Hits.* "I rest my case."

"Excuse me, but that was given to me by a very dear friend, and it happens to be a classic."

"A classic what?"

"Obviously, you have no appreciation for

nostalgia and have failed to recognize the sly, underlying social commentary of David Cassidy's rendition of 'I Think I Love You,' or the desperate sexual motivation that permeates the mood of 'Doesn't Somebody Want To Be Wanted.' But I'd be happy to discuss them with you."

"I bet you actually know the lyrics."

She managed to swallow the chuckle and began to wash the vegetables. "Naturally. During a brief, shining period in my youth, *I* was in a band."

"Right." He settled on B.B.

"Lead vocals and rhythm guitar. The Turbos." She smiled as he walked back to the counter. "Jesse—lead guitar—was into cars."

"You play guitar."

"Yes. Well, I played the guitar. A hot red Fender, which I imagine my mother still has in my old room—along with my toe shoes, my chemistry set, the sketches I made when I was going to be a fashion designer and the books I collected on animal husbandry before I realized that if I became a vet, I'd have to euthanize animals as well as play with them."

She laid a cutting board on the counter, selected the proper knife from her block. "They were all quests."

Fascinating, he thought. The woman was absolutely fascinating. "Fender guitars and toe shoes were quests?"

"I couldn't make up my mind what I wanted to be. Everything I tried was so much fun at first, then it was just work. Do you know how to slice peppers?"

"No. Don't you consider what you do now work, of a sort?"

She sighed and began to slice the peppers herself. "Yes, and it's not of a sort, either. It's a lot of work, but it's still fun. Don't you enjoy writing?"

"Rarely."

She looked up again. "Then why do you do it?"

"It won't let me do anything else. It's my only quest."

She nodded, switching to fat, white mushrooms. "It's like that for my mother. She never wanted to do anything but paint. Sometimes, when I watch her working, I can see how painful it is for her to have a vision and to have to pull out all her skills to transfer what she wants to communicate to canvas. But when she's finished, when it's right, she glows. The satisfaction, maybe even the shock of seeing what she's capable of doing, I suppose. It would be like that for you."

She glanced up, saw him studying her speculatively. "It always surprises you when I understand something other than what's right on the surface, doesn't it?"

He grabbed her hand before she could turn away. "If it does, it only means I'm the one who doesn't understand you. I'm likely to keep offending you until I do."

"I'm ridiculously easy to understand."

"No, that's what I thought. I was wrong. You're a maze, Cybil. With dozens of twists and turns and unexpected angles."

Her smile bloomed slowly, beautifully. "That's the nicest thing you've ever said to me."

"I'm not a nice man. You'd be smart to boot me out, lock your door and keep it that way."

"Being smart, I've figured that out for myself

already. However…" Gently, she laid a hand to his cheek. "You seem to be my new quest."

"Until it stops being fun and just becomes work?"

His eyes were so serious, she thought. And he was so ready to believe the worst. "McQuinn, you're already work, and you're still sitting in my kitchen." She smiled again. "Do you know how to slice carrots into pencil sticks?"

"I don't have a clue."

"Then watch and learn. Next time you're going to have to carry your weight." She peeled a carrot clean with a few quick, experienced strokes, then flicked a glancc up at him. "Am I still naked?"

"Do you want to be?"

She laughed and picked up her neglected wine.

It took a long time to cook a simple meal when you were distracted by conversation, by lingering looks, by seductive touches.

It took a long time to eat a simple meal when you were sliding lazily into love with the man across from you.

She recognized the signs—the erratic beating of the heart, the bubbling in the blood that was desire. When those were tangled so silkily around dreamy smiles and soft sighs, love was definitely a short trip away.

She wondered what it would be like when she reached it.

It took a long time to say good-night when you were floating on deep, dark kisses in the doorway.

And longer still to sleep when your body ached and your mind was full of dreams.

When she heard the faint drift of his music, she smiled and let it lull her to sleep.

Chapter 6

With his hair still wet from his morning shower, Preston sat at his own kitchen counter on one of Cybil's stools she'd insisted he borrow. He scanned the paper as he ate cold cereal and bananas because Cybil had pushed both on him once she'd gotten a look at his cupboards.

Even a kitchen klutz—which apparently meant him—could manage to pour milk onto cold cereal and slice a banana, she'd told him.

He'd decided against taking offense, though he didn't think he was quite as clumsy in the kitchen as she did. He'd managed to put a salad together, hadn't he? While she'd done something incredible and marvelous to a couple of pork chops.

The woman was one hell of a cook, he mused, and was rapidly spoiling his appetite for the quick slap-together sandwiches he often lived on.

It didn't seem to bother her that they hadn't gone out to dinner since that first meal she'd cooked for him. He imagined she would, before much longer, tire of preparing the evening meal and demand a restaurant.

People generally got itchy for a change of pace when the novelty wore off and routines became ruts.

And he supposed they already had a kind of routine. They kept to their separate corners during the day. Well, except for the couple of times she'd dropped by and persuaded him to go out. To the market, just for a walk, to buy a lamp.

He glanced back toward his living room, frowning at the whimsical bronze frog holding up a triangular-shaped lamp shade. He still wasn't sure how she'd talked him into buying such a thing, or into paying Mrs. Wolinsky for a secondhand recliner she'd wanted to get rid of.

And rightfully so, he decided. Who the hell wanted a green-and-yellow plaid recliner in their living room?

But somehow he had one—which despite its hideous looks was amazingly comfortable.

Of course if you had a chair and a lamp you needed a table. His was a sturdy Chippendale in desperate need of refinishing—and as Cybil had pointed out—a bargain because of it.

She just happened to have a friend who refinished furniture as a hobby, and would put him in touch.

She also just happened to have a friend who was a florist, which explained why there was a vase of cheerful yellow daisies on Preston's kitchen counter.

Another friend—of which Preston had decided she had a legion—painted New York street scenes and sold them on the sidewalk, and couldn't he use a couple of paintings to brighten up the walls?

He'd told her he didn't want to brighten anything, but there were now three very decent original watercolors on his wall.

She was already making noises about rugs.

He didn't know how she worked it, Preston thought, shaking his head as he went back to his breakfast. She just kept talking until you were pulling out your wallet or holding out your hand.

But they kept out of each other's way.

Well, there had been Saturday afternoon, when she'd invaded with buckets and mops and brooms and God knows what. If he was going to live in a place, she'd told him, at least it could be clean. And somehow he'd ended up spending three hours of a rainy afternoon when he should have been writing, scrubbing floors and chasing down dust.

Then again, he'd nearly gotten her into bed. Very nearly gotten her there, he remembered, when she'd stood in speechless shock at the state of his bedroom.

She'd gotten her voice back quickly enough and had launched into a lecture. He should have more respect for his workplace if not for his sleeping area, since they seemed to be one in the same. Why the hell did he keep the curtains drawn over the windows? Did he like caves? Did he have a religious objection to doing laundry?

He'd grabbed her out of self-defense and had stopped her mouth in the most satisfying of ways.

And if they hadn't tripped over a small mountain of laundry on the way to the bed, he doubted they'd have ended the afternoon with a trip to the cleaners.

Still, there were advantages, he thought. He appreciated a clean space, even though he rarely noticed a messy one. He liked tumbling into bed on freshly laundered sheets—though he would have preferred to tumble on them with Cybil. And it was hard to complain when you opened a cupboard and found actual food.

Even the sexual frustration was working for him. The writing was pouring out of it, and out of him. Maybe the play had taken a turn on him, focusing now more on a female character, one with a shining naïveté and enthusiasm. A woman alive with energy and optimism. And one who'd be seduced by and damaged by a man who had none of those things inside him. A man who wouldn't be able to stop himself from taking them from her, then leaving her shattered.

He saw the parallels well enough between what he created and what was, but he refused to worry about it.

He sipped his coffee, reminding himself to ask Cybil why his always tasted faintly of swamp water, and turned to the comic section to see what she'd been up to.

He skimmed it, frowned, then went back to the first section and read it again.

She was already at work, her window open, because spring had decided to be kind. A lovely warm breeze wafted through along with the chaos of street noise.

After her sheet of paper was set and scaled, she set her T-square back in its place in the custom-built tool area she'd designed to suit herself. She tilted her head, facing the first blank section. It was double the size of what would appear in the dailies in a couple of weeks. She already had it in her mind—the setup, the situation and the punch line that would comprise those five windows and give the readership their morning chuckle over coffee.

The elusive Mr. Mysterious, now known as Quinn, huddled in his dim cave, writing the Great American Novel. Sexy, cranky, irresistible Quinn, so serious, so intense in his own little world he was completely unaware that Emily was crouched on his fire escape, peering through the narrow chink of his perpetually drawn curtains, struggling to read his work in progress through a pair of binoculars.

Amused at herself—because in her own way Cybil knew her subtle little probes and questions on how his play was going were the more civilized version of her counterpart's voyeurism, she settled down to lightly sketch her professional interpretation of the man across the hall.

She exaggerated ruthlessly, his good points and his bad. The tall, muscular body, the ruggedly chiseled looks, the cool eyes. His rudeness, his humor and his perpetual bafflement with the world Emily lived in.

Poor guy, she thought, he doesn't have a clue what to do with her.

When the buzzer sounded, she tucked her pencil behind her ear, thinking Jody had forgotten her key.

She stopped to top off her coffee cup on the way. "Just hang on. Coming."

Then she opened the door and experienced one more rapid meltdown. His hair was just a little damp and he wasn't wearing a shirt. Boy, oh, boy, just look at those pecs, she thought, and barely resisted licking her lips.

His jeans were faded, his feet bare, and his face—his face was so wonderfully serious and sober.

"Hi." She managed to make it sound bright and easy while she pictured herself biting him. "You run out of soap in the shower? Need to borrow some?"

"What? No." He'd forgotten he was only half-dressed. "I want to ask you about this," he continued, lifting the paper.

"Sure, come on in." It would be safe, she told herself. Jody would be there any minute and stop her from jumping Preston. "Why don't you get some coffee and come up? I'm working and it's rolling pretty well."

"I don't want to interrupt, but—"

"Not much does," she said cheerfully over her shoulder as she started up the stairs. "There's cinnamon bagels if you want one."

"No." Hell, he thought, and ended up pouring a cup of coffee and taking a bagel after all.

He hadn't been upstairs before, since he'd never come over when she was working. He tormented himself by glancing into her bedroom, studying the big bed with its bold blue cover and sumptuous mountain of jewel-toned pillows, the slim rods of the white iron headboard where he could imagine trapping her hands under his as he finally did everything he wanted with her. To her.

It smelled of her, fresh, female, with seductive undertones of vanilla.

She kept rose petals in a bowl, a book beside the bed and candles in the window.

"Find everything?" she called out.

He shook himself. "Yeah. Listen, Cybil…" He stepped into her studio. "God, how do you work with all that noise?"

She barely glanced up. "What noise? Oh, that." She continued to sketch, using a new pencil, as she'd forgotten the one behind her ear. "Sort of like background music. Half the time I don't hear it."

The room looked efficient and creative with its neat shelves holding both supplies and clever tchotchkes. He recognized the work of the sidewalk artist in one of the paintings on her wall, and the genius of her mother in two others.

There was a complex and fascinating metal sculpture in the corner, a little clutch of violets tucked into a glass inkwell and a cozy divan heaped with more pillows against the wall.

But she didn't look efficient, bent over the big slanted board with her legs folded up under her, the toenails of her bare feet painted pink, a pencil behind one ear and a gold hoop in the other.

She looked scattered, and sexy.

Curious, he walked around to peer over her shoulder. An act that, he admitted, had anyone dared to try on him would have earned the offender a quick and painful death.

"What are all the blue lines for?"

"Scaling, perspective. Takes a little math before you can get down to business. I work in five windows for the dailies," she continued, sketching easily. "I have to set them on paper like this, work out the theme, the gag, the hit, so that the strip can move from start to finish in five connected beats."

Satisfied, she moved to the next section. "I sketch it in first, just need to see how it hangs—you'd say a draft, where you get the story line down, then decide where it needs to be punched up. I'll give it more details, fiddle a bit before I switch to pen and ink."

He frowned, focusing on the first sketch. "Is that supposed to be me?"

"Hmm. Why don't you pull up a stool. You're blocking the light."

"What is she doing there?" Ignoring the suggestion, he tapped a finger on the second window. "Spying on me. You're spying on me?"

"Don't be ridiculous—you don't even have a fire escape outside your bedroom." She looked into her mirror, made several faces that left him staring at her, then started on the third section.

"What about this?" he demanded, rapping the paper on her shoulder.

"What about it? God, you smell fabulous." Pleasing herself, she turned and sniffed him. "What kind of soap is that?"

"Are you going to have this guy take a shower next?" When she pursed her lips in obvious consideration, Preston shook his head. "No. There has to be a line. I was oddly amused when you introduced this parody of me into the script, but—"

He broke off as he heard her front door open and slam shut. "Who's that?"

"That would be Jody and Charlie. So you've gotten a kick out of the new guy?" She stopped sketching and shifted to smile up at him. "I wondered, because you hadn't mentioned it before. You know, some people don't even recognize themselves. They just have no self-awareness, I suppose, but I thought you'd see it if you happened to read the strip. Hi, Jody. There's Charlie."

"Hi." It wasn't an easy matter, even for a happily married woman, to keep her tongue from falling out when she was so suddenly and unexpectedly faced with a well-muscled, naked male chest. "Uh, hi. Are we interrupting?"

"No, Preston just had some questions about the strip."

"I love the new guy. He's really got Emily in a spin. I can't wait to see what happens next." She broke into a wide grin as Charlie exploded out a "Da!" and reached for Preston.

"He calls every man he sees 'Da.' Chuck's a little put out by it, but Charlie's just a guy's guy, you know."

"Right." Absently, Preston ran a hand over Charlie's downy brown hair. "I just want to get something straight about how this thing is going," he began, turning back to Cybil.

"Da!" Charlie said again, arms extended hopefully, smile sleepy.

"Just how close to reality do you work?" Preston asked, automatically taking the baby and settling him on his shoulder.

Cybil's heart simply melted. "You like babies."

"No, I toss them out of third-story windows at every opportunity," he said impatiently, then shook his head when Jody squeaked. "Relax.

He's fine. What I want to know is this business here." Shifting the baby, he dropped the comic section on her board.

"Oh, the 'no scale' bit. This is really part one. They'll run the second half of it tomorrow. I think it works."

"Chuck and I fell over laughing when we read it this morning," Jody put in, relaxed again as she watched Preston absently patting the now-sleeping baby.

"You've got these two women here—"

"Emily and Cari."

"I know who they are by now," Preston muttered, narrowing his eyes at both women. "They're discussing—they're rating, for God's sake—the way Quinn kissed Emily a couple days ago."

"Uh-huh. Chuck laughed?" Cybil wanted to know. "I wondered if men would get it or if it would just hit with women."

"Oh, yeah, he died over it."

"Pardon me." With what he considered admirable restraint, Preston held up a hand. "I'd like to know if the two of you sit around here discussing your various sexual encounters and then rating them on a scale of one to ten before you then give the American public a good chuckle over it with their corn flakes."

"Discussing them?" Eyes wide and innocent, Cybil stared up at Preston. "Honestly, McQuinn, this is a comic strip. You're taking it too seriously."

"So all this about the no scale is just a bit?"

"What else?"

He studied her face. "I wouldn't like to think that when I finally get you into bed, I'm going to read about my performance in five sections in the morning paper."

"Oh, my. Oh, well." Jody patted a hand on her heart. "I think I'll just take Charlie and go put him down for his nap." She eased him out of Preston's arms and hurried out.

"McQuinn." Cybil smiled, tapped her pencil. "I have a feeling that event would be worth the full Sunday spread."

"Is that a threat or a joke?"

When she only laughed, he spun her stool around, then knocked the air out of her lungs with a fierce and demanding kiss. "Tell your friend to go away, and we'll find out."

"No, I'm keeping her. She's all that stopped me from biting your throat when you came in."

"Are you trying to drive me crazy?"

"Not really. It's kind of a side effect." Her pulse had gone from slow shuffle to manic tap dance. "You've got to go. I've finally found a distraction I can't work through. And you're it."

Seeing no reason he should go crazy alone, he leaned down one last time and took her mouth. "When you speak of this—" he caught her bottom lip between his teeth, drawing it erotically through them "—and I expect you will, be accurate."

He walked to the doorway, turning back in time to see her shudder. "No scale?" he said, realizing he suddenly found it not just amusing but gratifying.

When she managed to do nothing more than make one helpless gesture with her hands, he laughed. And was still grinning when he jogged down her steps and out the door.

"Safe?" Jody whispered, poking her head into the doorway.

"Oh, God, God, Jody, what am I going to do

here?" Shaken, Cybil stabbed the second pencil behind her ear, knocked the first out of place, and didn't even bother to curse. "I thought I had it all figured out. I mean what's wrong with easing yourself into what promises to be a blistering, roof-raising affair with an incredibly intense, gorgeous, interesting man?"

"Let me think." Holding up a finger, Jody strolled in and picked up the coffee Preston had never touched. "Okay, I've got it. Nothing. The answer to that question is nothing."

"And if you're a little bit in love with him, that only sweetens the deal, right?"

"Absolutely. Otherwise it's fun but sort of like eating too much chocolate at one sitting. You enjoy it when it's going on, then you feel a little queasy and ashamed."

"But what if you went all the way in. What do you do when you've gone over the brink?"

Jody set down the coffee. "You went over the brink?"

"Just now."

"Oh, honey." All sympathy, Jody wrapped her arms around Cybil and rocked. "It's all right. It had to happen sooner or later."

"I know, but I always thought it would be later."

"We all do."

"He won't want me to be in love with him. It'll just annoy him." Turning her face to Jody's shoulder, she let out a shaky breath. "I'm not too happy about it myself, but I'll get used to it."

"Sure you will. Poor Frank." With a sigh, Jody patted Cybil's shoulder, then stepped back. "He never really had a shot, did he?"

"Sorry."

"Oh, well." Jody dismissed her favorite cousin with an absent flick of the wrist. "What are you going to do?"

"I don't know. I guess running and hiding's out."

"That's for wimps."

"Yeah. Wimps. How about pretending it'll go away?"

"That's for morons."

Cybil drew a bracing breath. "How about shopping?"

"Now you're talking." On a quick salute, Jody headed for the door. "I'll see if Mrs. Wolinsky will watch Charlie, then we'll handle this problem like real women."

She bought a new dress. A slinky length of black sin that made Jody roll her eyes and declare, "The man's a goner," when Cybil tried it on.

She bought new shoes. Mile-high heels as thin as honed scalpels.

She bought new lingerie. The kind women wear when they expect it to be seen by a man who'll then be compelled to rip it off.

And she imagined Preston's wide hands and long fingers peeling the silky-as-cobwebs hose down her legs.

Then there were flowers to choose, candles, wine.

Marketing for a meal she would design to tease the senses and whet the palate for a more primitive kind of appetite.

By the time she got home she was loaded down, and she was calm.

There was a scene to be set, and doing so gave her focus. Because she wanted to take the rest of the day to prepare, because she needed it to be perfect, she wrote a note to Preston and stuck it to her door.

Then she locked herself in, drew a deep breath and took everything up to the bedroom.

She arranged tender lilies and fragrant rosebuds in vases, in bowls, and set them on tables, the dresser, the windowsills. Then she grouped candles, all white, a trio here, a single there, a half-dozen scented tealights on a circle of mirrored glass.

Some she lit so the room would fill with soft light and gentle fragrance while she worked.

She unwrapped two slender-stemmed wineglasses, placed them just so on the low table in front of the curved wicker chaise. Reminded herself to chill the wine.

Facing the bed, she stopped, considered. Would turning down the duvet and sheets be too obvious? Then she laughed at herself. Why stop now?

When it was done, when she could look around the room and see there was nothing that wasn't as she needed it to be, she went down to make the early preparations for the meal she intended to cook.

She listened, hoping he'd begin to play so that some of him would come inside her rooms with her. But his apartment remained silent.

With careful deliberation she chose music for mood, arranging CDs in her changer.

Satisfied, she went back up, laid her new dress on the bed, shivered in anticipation as she set the black lace bra and the blatantly provocative matching garter belt beside it and imagined what it would feel like to wear them.

Powerful, she decided. Secretive and certain.

She shivered again, thrilling to the clutch of lust deep in her center, then went to draw a hot, frothy bath.

She poured wine, lit more candles to promote the mood, before she slipped into the tub. And closing her eyes, she imagined Preston's hands, rather than the frothy water, on her.

Nearly an hour later, she was slathering every inch of her body with cream, sliding her fingers along to make certain her skin was silky and scented, when Preston tugged her note off the front door: McQuinn, I've got plans. I'll see you later. Cybil

Plans? Plans? She had plans when he'd worked himself into a turmoil over her all day?

He read the note again, furious with both of them, as he hadn't been able to get the image of spending yet another foolish evening with her out of his head.

For God's sake, he'd gone out and bought her flowers. He hadn't bought flowers for a woman since...

He crumpled the note in his hand. What else could he expect? Women were, first and foremost, tuned to their own agenda. He'd known it, accepted it, and if he'd let himself forget that single relevant detail with Cybil, he had no one to blame but himself.

She'd see him later?

It appeared she was a game player after all. But he didn't have to step up to bat.

He turned, marched back into his apartment, where he tossed the lilacs that had inexplicably reminded him of her on the kitchen counter. He flipped her balled note across the room, picked up his sax and stalked out to work off his temper at Delta's.

At exactly seven-thirty, Cybil took the stuffed mushrooms she'd slaved over out of the oven. The table was set for two, with more candles, more flowers precisely arranged. There was a wonderfully colorful avocado-and-tomato salad chilling along with the wine.

Once they'd enjoyed their appetizers and first course, she intended to destroy him with her seafood crepes.

If all went according the plan, they'd polish off the meal with icy champagne and fresh raspberries and cream. In bed.

"Okay, Cybil."

She took off her apron, marched to the mirror to check the fit and line of the dress. She slipped on her heels, added another dash of perfume, then gave her reflection a bracing smile.

"Let's go get him."

She sauntered across the hall, pressed his buzzer, then waited with her heart hammering. Shifting from foot to foot, she buzzed again.

"How could you not be home? How *could* you? Didn't you get the note? You must have. It's not on the door, is it? Didn't I specifically say I'd see you later?"

Groaning, she thumped her fist against the door. Then she jerked upright and blinked.

"I said I had plans. Oh, my God, you didn't

get it, did you, you thick-headed jerk? *You're* the plans. Oh, hell." She made a dash back through her open door for her key, realized she didn't have anywhere to put it. With a shrug, she stuck it into her bra rather than waste time running upstairs for a bag.

In thirty seconds flat, she was risking a broken neck by running down the stairs.

"Woman trouble, sugar lips?"

Preston looked over at Delta as he took a break to wet his throat. "No woman. No trouble."

"This is Delta." She tapped a finger to his cheek. "Every night this week you come in here late and you play like a man who's got a woman on his mind. And this man doesn't much mind having her there. Now tonight, you come in early and you're playing like a man who's got trouble with the woman. Did you have a fight with that pretty little girl?"

"No. We've both got other things to do."

"Still holding you off, is she?" She laughed, but not without sympathy. "Some woman take more romance than others."

"It has nothing to do with romance."

"Maybe that's your problem." Delta wrapped an arm around his shoulders and squeezed. "Do you ever buy her flowers? Tell her she has beautiful eyes."

"No." Damn it, he had brought her flowers. She hadn't bothered to stick around to take them. "It's sex, not a courtship."

"Oh, sweetheart. You want one, you better do the other with a woman like that."

"That's why I'm better off without a woman like that. I want it simple." He picked up the sax, lifted a brow. "Now, are you going to let me play, or do you want to give me more advice on my love life?"

With a shake of her head, she stepped back. "When you have a love life, *cher,* I'll have advice."

He blew off a riff, listening to the music inside his head. Inside his blood. He let the notes come, but the music didn't take his mind off her. He could use that, as well, he told himself. Here, where sharing was a pleasure. Not with words, where it was often pain.

The notes slipped out, throbbed in the air, sobbed into a wail.

And she walked in the door.

Her eyes, full of secrets, met his through the haze of smoke, held. And the smile she sent him as she slid into a chair made his palms go damp. She moistened her lips, trailed a finger up from the center of the low bodice of the slinky black dress to the base of her throat. And back again.

He watched, his blood swimming, as she crossed long, long legs with a movement so slow, so studied, it had to be deliberate. Surely the way she ran her hand from calf to knee to thigh was designed to make a man's gaze follow the movement.

His did, and his pulse leaped like a wolf on the hunt.

She sat through the song, leaning back in the chair, hooking one arm provocatively over the back. When the notes faded, she traced the tip of her tongue lazily over those hot red lips.

Then she rose, her gaze still locked with his as the music pumped. She ran a hand down her hip, turned on those man-killer heels and started back out. She glanced over her shoulder, sent him a sultry invitation with no more than a lift of eyebrow and left the door swinging behind her.

The oath that came out of his mouth when he lowered the sax was absolutely reverent.

"You going after that, brother?"

Preston crouched to push his sax into its case. "Do I look stupid, André?"

"No." André chuckled and kept on playing. "No, you don't."

Chapter 7

She was waiting on the sidewalk when he came out, standing in the white wash of a streetlight with one hand resting on a cocked hip, her head angled, her lips curved in the barest hint of a smile. It made him think of a photograph, some arty shot perfectly framed and cropped for a classy magazine.

Sex in black and white.

He started toward her, taking more in the closer he came. The short, whiskey-colored hair sleeked to frame her face. The short black dress sleeked to frame her body.

No jewelry to distract the eye.

Mile-high heels designed to showcase mile-long legs.

The only color was on those huge green eyes under sooty lashes and the siren red of her mouth. A mouth, he noted, that was curved in smug, female satisfaction.

He was three steps away when her scent reached out like a crooked finger and beckoned him the rest of the way.

"Hello, neighbor." She purred it—one more hot bullet to his loins.

He tilted his head, lifted a brow. "Change of plans...neighbor?"

"I hope not." She took the last step, moving into him, deliberately sliding her hands up his sides, over his shoulders, around his neck. Her body fit suggestively to his as she purred again.

Then she laughed, shook her head. "You were the plans, you knothead."

She wondered if it was the announcement or the mild insult that had his eyes narrowing in speculation.

"Is that so?"

"McQuinn." She tilted her head, brought her mouth a whisper from his. Then, with her eyes on his, slowly licked. "Didn't I tell you you'd be the first to know?"

"Yeah." With his free hand he cupped her neck, keeping that wet red mouth tantalizingly close to his. "How fast can you walk in those heels?"

She laughed again, just a little breathlessly now. "Not very. But we've got all night, don't we?"

"It might just take longer than that." He stepped back, and after a moment, held out a hand for hers. "Where did you get the lethal weapon? The dress," he added when she gave him a blank look.

"Oh, this old thing." This time her laugh was warm and rich. "I bought it today, thinking of you. And when I put it on tonight, I was thinking of what it was going to be like when you took it off me."

"You must have been practicing," he said when he could manage to form words again. "Because you're damn good at this."

"Actually, I'm making it up as I go along."

"Don't stop on my account."

It was amazing, she thought, that a balmy spring evening could suddenly seem as sultry as summer in the Tropics. "Sorry I wasn't more specific in my note. I had a lot on my mind." She turned, delighted that the heels brought her eye level with his mouth. "A lot of you on my mind."

"It pissed me off." It didn't seem so hard to admit it.

"Pardon me if I find that very flattering. When I knocked on your door and you didn't answer, I had essentially the same reaction. I spent a lot of time getting ready for you. You can be flattered."

"It must have taken a while to paint on what there is of that dress."

"Not just that." She'd managed to keep her heartbeat fairly steady, but as she paused at the entrance to their building, it began to plunge and kick. "I made dinner."

"You did?" He wasn't just flattered, he realized. He wasn't just aroused. He was touched.

"A fairly fabulous one, if I do say so myself," she added, backing into the building. "With a sassy little white wine to set it off—and an elegant and icy champagne to go with dessert."

She led the way into the elevator, pushed the button for three, then leaned back against the wall. "Which I thought we could enjoy in bed."

He kept a step away, knowing if he touched her they wouldn't be leaving the elevator for a very long time. "Anything else I should know about these plans of yours?"

"Oh, I don't think you're going to need me to write anything down." She stepped off the elevator, tossed one of those slow smiles over her shoulder and strolled to her door.

He thought if he managed to get inside without exploding, he'd show her he could make plans of his own. "Key?"

"Hmm." Keeping her eyes on his, she slid a finger under the deep scoop of her bodice, touched metal and watched his gaze drop, heat, linger. "Gee." She slid her finger up again, circled it lazily at the base of her throat. "I can't seem to find it. Maybe you can get it for me."

He decided he had news for medical science. It was possible to remain conscious and upright after all the blood had drained out of your head.

He trailed his finger along the inviting swell above the black silk—felt her shiver, heard the catchy intake of her breath. Then dipped down, taking his time, gliding his finger lazily over heated flesh, gently abrading her nipple until her eyes clouded and closed.

"I'd say you're the one who's been practicing," she managed, and made him smile.

"I'm just making it up as I go along."

"Mmm-hmm. Don't stop on my account."

He didn't intend to. Not for hours. "Looks like I found it," he murmured, hooking the key.

"Yeah." She let out a long, long breath. "I just knew you would."

He slid the key home, released locks. "Ask me in, Cybil."

"Come in."

He pushed open the door, backed her inside. Reaching behind, he locked the door. Clamping his hands on her hips, he kept walking.

"Dinner?"

"Can wait." He lifted the phone off the hook as they passed it.

"The wine?"

"Later. Much later." Her heels bumped into the bottom step. This time he smiled. "Keep going."

On legs that had gone weak, she moved up the stairs with her hands braced on his shoulders.

"Ask me to touch you."

"Touch me." She sighed as his hands traveled up.

"Ask me to taste you."

"Taste me." And moaned as his mouth brushed over the rise of her breasts.

When they reached the bedroom door, his teeth scraped along her throat, her jaw, and left her mouth aching for attention.

"Kiss me."

"I will." But he only teased the corners of her lips with the tip of his tongue. "I want the light."

"No, I have candles. They're everywhere." She broke free to grab a matchbook, then fumbled. "I can't. I'm shaking. Isn't that ridiculous?"

He took the matches from her and danced his fingertips along her thigh. "I want you to. Don't move," he ordered, then worked his way around the room setting the candles alight.

The glow shimmered. The scent whispered.

Tossing the matches aside, he moved back to where she stood, her eyes huge and full of nerves, needs and candlelight.

"Now." His hands slid around her waist, down. "Ask me to take you."

She kept her eyes on his. "Take me."

His mouth captured hers, plundered, rocking her with the first punch of the power they'd built between them. She grabbed on, as much to add to the storm as ride it. This was what she wanted, this bold, blistering, battering heat. The crash of senses, the war of needs.

"I want you." She raced wild kisses over his face. "I want you in bed."

Then she gasped as he whirled her around, dragged her back against him. It stunned her to see them reflected in the mirror, to see the gleam of desire in his gaze as it traveled down her body.

"We have all night," he reminded her. "Watch."

He dipped his head to the curve of her neck

and shoulder, sharp little bites that had the first helpless sounds catching in her throat.

She watched his hands travel up, saw them, felt them cup her breasts, squeeze, release, slide over silk, his fingers sliding under it, tugging the material. She braced for him to rip.

Then shuddered as he simply let his hands glide over her again, then down. She cried out in aroused shock as he pressed against her center.

His head lifted, his teeth catching the lobe of her ear as their gazes met in the mirror. She'd driven him crazy when she'd walked into the club. He intended to return the favor.

"Tell me you want more."

Her muscles had gone lax, her bones to jelly. "Preston."

He traced his fingers up and down her thighs, felt the muscles quiver and the flesh heat. "Tell me you want more."

"God." Her head fell back on his shoulder as she fought for air. "I want more."

"So do I."

He moved from silky hose to silky flesh, torturing himself. Her scent was destroying him, the feel of her urging him to take all of her. But he drew it out, even as his own breath became labored; he held back the animal pacing inside him.

Because when he let it go, he knew it would devour them both.

He nipped his way around the back of her neck, her shoulders, while he tugged down the zipper of her dress. He peeled it off her, then bit back a groan.

Sex in black and white, he thought again.

Even through the haze of desire she saw his eyes change. Saw something dangerous flash into them. It shocked her to realize that was what she wanted. The danger, the risk, the glory of breaking whatever choke chain he had on his control.

Power swirled into her as she covered his hands with hers and guided them over her. "I bought this today," she whispered, holding his hands to her breasts. "So you could rip it off me tonight."

She curled her fingers with his, nudged them over the thin silk connecting the lace. And let out one sharp gasp when he yanked the dress apart.

And with that single movement, he broke.

He spun her around, his mouth ravishing hers now, his hands close to brutal as he dragged her to the bed.

He was going to eat her alive, and couldn't stop it. He felt her arch and buck when his hand covered her. Heard her choked scream as he drove her over the first ragged edge. Then he was tearing at silk and lace, desperate for more.

He feasted on her breasts, the firm fragrant swell of them, while her heart hammered against his mouth. Her hands drove him wild as they pulled at his shirt, as her nails scraped down his back.

Her mouth was as greedy as his, her hands as rough and impatient as they tugged and dragged at his jeans. And when they closed around him, fire burst in his blood.

She rolled with him, tangling in the sheets she'd so carefully smoothed. Panting, shuddering, she wrapped herself around him, bowed up in urgent demand.

When he drove into her, heat into heat, the explosion of pleasure was huge, a fast, hard, turbulent wave that drenched the skin and swamped the soul. With one throaty moan, she matched him for speed and fury.

More was all he could think. He had to have more of her. Clamping her hands on the slim iron poles of the headboard, he plunged deeper. She arched, accepted. Mad on the pleasure of her, he watched her face, absorbing every flicker of shock and delight as he took her higher, and faster, then over so that she sobbed out his name, so that her eyes went dark and blind.

As her body melted under his, he let himself pour into her. Surrendered himself.

His hands continued to hold hers on the rungs, though her fingers had gone limp. His body continued to cover hers while she quaked. He stayed inside her. Mated.

"Are we still breathing?"

He turned his head, felt the pulse in her throat scrambling. "Your heart's still beating."

"Good, that's good. Is yours?"

"Seems to be."

"Okay, then it's probably safe for us to stay

here like this for the next five or ten years. I'm pretty sure I'll be able to move by then."

He lifted his head. Though she kept her eyes closed, Cybil was aware she was being studied, imagined that clear blue and focused gaze. And smiled. "I seduced the hell out of you, McQuinn. It was awfully nice of you to return the favor."

"No problem. It was the least I could do."

"Nobody ever made me feel like this before." She opened her eyes. "No one ever touched me this way."

She saw her mistake immediately. The way his eyes shuttered, the way he retreated from the intimacy. If it was light, if it was sexy, if it was dangerous, he was with her. But there was to be no tenderness, no heart, no slippery sentiment, to change the balance.

It made her ache for both of them.

"You've got great hands." She made her smile sassy as she wiggled her fingers under his. "Definitely major-league hands."

"You've got some real contenders yourself." He rolled onto his back, relieved and annoyed with himself for feeling that deep inner jolt when she'd looked at him with so much dazzled emotion in her eyes.

He wasn't going to let things shift into that area between them. Because once it did, it was over. That part of him that was hope and heart had long ago been calcified.

She wanted to curl into him, to curve her body into the warmth of his, but imagined that was another taboo. Keep it simple, she warned herself, or he'll walk right out the door.

So she sat up, instead, flicked her fingers through her disordered hair. "I think that wine would go down well right now, don't you?"

"Oh, yeah." He skimmed his fingers along her calf, because he had to touch, had to keep that connection. "You mentioned something about dinner."

"McQuinn, I have an amazing meal in store for you." She leaned down to give him a careless kiss. "Everything's done but the crepes— seafood crepes, which I will whip up in front of your astonished eyes."

"You're going to cook?"

"Mmm-hmm."

He watched her slide out of bed, walk to the

closet on legs that had his blood stirring again. "What's that for?"

"This? It's called a robe," she said with a laugh as she slipped into it. "It's often used to cover nakedness."

He got up, crossed to her and tugged the belt loose again. "Take it off."

A quick thrill shimmied down her spine. "I thought you wanted dinner."

"I do. And I want to watch you cook it."

"Then—oh." She laughed again and pulled the robe together. "I am not cooking crepes naked. That little fantasy of yours is doomed."

He didn't think so. "Actually, I was wondering if you had any more of…" He turned to the bed, found what was left of the lacy black garter belt. "This sort of thing."

Surprised, then intrigued, she lifted her eyebrows. "No intelligent shopper buys only one. I have another little ensemble in red. Break-your-heart, tart red."

His smile spread slowly as he tossed the black lace aside. "Why don't you put it on? I'm really hungry."

* * *

Preparing crepes in sexy underwear was not without its risks. Cybil discovered just what it was like to be ravished against the pantry door.

Amazing.

And plundered on the living-room rug.

Incredible.

And being savaged under the hot, beating spray of the shower was an experience she would be more than willing to repeat.

Through the hours of the night he'd reached for her, thrilled her, had never seemed quite able to get enough of her. Or she of him. They'd been so completely in tune, so utterly together, that at times it had seemed his heart had beat inside hers.

The candles had gutted out in their own fragrant pools, and light had been seeping softly through the windows when she'd fallen into an exhausted sleep.

Only to wake alone.

She knew it shouldn't hurt her that he hadn't slept with her, hadn't woken with her. It wasn't to be like that between them. She knew that, ac-

cepted that. There would be no soft and foolish
words between them, no baring of souls.

The border of intimacy stopped at the physi-
cal, with his side of it walled thick. Her heart
was her own problem, not his.

How could he know she'd never given herself
so absolutely to any other man? Why should he
be expected to know that the primitive power of
their desire for each other was driven by love on
her side?

She rubbed her tired eyes and ordered herself
up and out of bed.

She'd walked into the relationship with her
eyes open, she thought as she tidied up the bedroom. She'd known its limitations. His limitations. They could be together, enjoy each other,
as long as certain lines weren't crossed.

Well, that was fine. She wasn't going to pine
and sigh over it. She was in charge of her own
emotions; she was responsible for her own actions; and she was hardly going to mope around
because she was involved with an exciting, fascinating, interesting man.

"Damn it!" She hurled her shoes into the
closet. "Damn it, damn it, damn it!"

Cybil leaped on the bed, grabbed the phone. She had to tell someone, talk to someone. And when it was this vital, there was really only one someone.

"Mama? Mama, I'm in love," she said, then burst into wild tears.

Preston's fingers flew over the keyboard. He'd had less than three hours' sleep, but his system was revved, his mind clear as crystal. His first major play had been wrenched out of him, every word a wound. But this was pouring out, streaming like wine out of a magic bottle that had only been waiting to be decanted.

It was so fully alive. And for the first time in longer than he could remember, so was he.

He could see it all perfectly, the sets, the staging, the characters and everything inside them. The doomed, the damned, the triumphant.

A world in three acts.

There was an energy here, inside these people who formed on the page and lived on the stage already set inside his head. He knew them, knew how their hearts would leap and how they would break.

The thread of hope that ran through their lives hadn't been planned, but it was there, woven through and tangled so that he found himself riding on it with them.

He wrote until he ran dry; then, disoriented, glanced around the room. It was dark but for the lamp he'd switched on and the steady glow from his computer screen. He hadn't a clue what time it was—what day, for that matter. But his neck and shoulders were stiff, his stomach empty, and the coffee in the cup on his desk looked faintly revolting.

Standing, he worked out the worst of the kinks, then walked to the window, pushed open the curtains. There was a hell of a spring storm going on. He hadn't noticed. Now he watched the flashing of lightning, the scurry of desperate pedestrians rushing to appointments or shelter.

The entrepreneur on the corner was doing a brisk business in the umbrellas, which no one in New York seemed to own for longer than it took the pavement to dry.

He wondered if Cybil was looking out her window, watching the same scene. What she would think of it, how she would turn something so simple and ordinary as a thunderstorm in the city into the bright and ridiculous.

She'd use the Umbrella Man, he decided, work up an entire biography for him, give the figure in black slicker and hood a name, a background, a personality full of quirks. And the anonymous street vendor would become part of her world.

She had such a gift for drawing people into her world.

He was in it now, Preston mused. He hadn't been able to stop himself from opening that colorful door and stepping inside the confusion, the delights, the energy.

She didn't seem to understand he didn't belong there.

When he was inside, when he was surrounded by her, it seemed as though he could stay. That if he let it, life could be just that simple and extraordinary.

Like a storm in the city, he thought. But storms pass.

He'd nearly let himself sink into it that morning. Nearly let himself sink in and stay in that warm bed, with that warm body that had turned to curl around him in sleep.

She'd looked so...soft, he thought now. So welcoming. What had moved through him as he'd watched her in that fragile light had been a different kind of hunger. One that yearned to hold, to sigh out all the troubles and doubts and hold on to dreams.

It had been safer for both of them to leave her sleeping.

He flicked the curtains closed and walked downstairs.

He started fresh coffee, foraged for food, toyed with the idea of a nap.

But he thought of her, and of the night, and knew the restlessness inside him wouldn't allow him to rest.

What was she doing over there?

He had no business knocking on her door, interrupting her work just because his was finished for now. Just because the drum of rain made him feel edgy and alone. Just because he wanted her.

He liked being alone, he reminded himself as

he prowled the living area. He needed the edge for his work.

He wanted to sit with her and watch the rain. To make slow, lazy love with her while it pounded the streets and sidewalks and co-cooned them from everything but each other.

Wanted her, he admitted, just a little too much for comfort.

He told himself it was safe enough to want. It was crossing the line from want to need that was dangerous. Just how close, he wondered, was he already skirting that very thin, very shaky line?

When a woman got inside a man this way, it changed him, left him wide-open so that he made mistakes and exposed pieces of himself better left alone.

She wasn't Pamela. He wasn't so blind he believed every woman was a liar and a cheat and cold as stone. If he'd ever known anyone with less potential for cruelty and deceit, it was Cybil Campbell.

But that didn't change the bottom line.

From want to need to love were short, skidding steps. Once a man had taken the fall and ended up broken, he learned to keep his balance at all costs. He didn't want the desperation, the vulnerability, the loss of self that went hand in hand with genuine intimacy. And he'd stopped believing himself capable of those things.

Which meant there was nothing to worry about, he told himself, sipping his coffee and staring at his door as if he could see through it and through the one across the hall. She wasn't asking for anything more than passion, companionship, enjoyment.

Exactly as he was.

She was perfectly aware the arrangement was temporary.

He'd be gone in a few weeks, and their lives would go comfortably in other directions. She with her crowds of friends, he with his contented solitude.

He'd set his cup down with a violent snap before he realized the idea annoyed him.

They could still see each other from time to time, he told himself as he began to pace again. His house in Connecticut was a reasonable commute from the city. Isn't that why he'd chosen it in the first place?

He came into the city often enough. There was no reason he couldn't make it more often.

Until she got involved with someone else, he thought, jamming his hands in his pockets. Why should a woman like that wait around for him to breeze in and out of her life?

And that was fine, too, he decided as his temper began to rumble like the thunder outside. Who was asking her to wait around? She could damn well hook herself up with any idiot her interfering friends tossed at her.

But not, by God, while he was still across the hall.

He strode to her door, intending to make a few things clear. And opened it just in time to watch Cybil launch herself joyfully into the arms of a tall man with sun-streaked brown hair.

"Still the prettiest girl in New York," he said in a voice that hinted of beignets and chicory. "Give me a kiss."

And as she did, lavishly, Preston wondered which method of murder would be most satisfying.

Chapter 8

"Matthew! Why didn't you tell me you were coming? When did you get in? How long are you staying? Oh, I'm so happy to see you! You're all wet. Come inside, take off your jacket—when are you going to buy a new one? This one looks like it's been through a war."

He only laughed, hefted her off her feet and kissed her again. "You still never shut up."

"I babble when I'm happy. When are you— oh, Preston." She beamed at him out of eyes shining with joy. "I didn't see you there."

"Obviously." Bare hands, he thought, would

be the most satisfying. He would simply take the guy with the smug brown eyes and the scarred leather jacket apart piece by piece. And feed each one to Cybil. "Don't let me interrupt the reunion."

"It's great, isn't it? Matthew, this is Preston McQuinn."

"McQuinn?" Matthew ran his tongue around his teeth. He was fairly sure the man braced in the hallway wanted to break them. "The playwright. I caught your work the last time I was in the city. Cyb cried buckets. I practically had to carry her out of the theater."

"I wasn't that bad."

"Yes, you were. Of course, you used to tear up during greeting-card commercials, so you're an easy mark."

"That's ridiculous, and—oh, my phone. Hang on a minute." She darted inside, leaving the men eyeing each other narrowly.

"I'm a sculptor," Matthew said in the same lazy drawl. "And since I really need my hands to work, I'll tell you I'm Cybil's brother before I offer to shake."

"Brother?" The murderous gleam shifted

but didn't quite fade. "Not much family resemblance."

"Not especially. Want to see my ID, McQuinn?"

"That was Mrs. Wolinsky," Cybil announced as she dashed back. "She saw you come in but couldn't get to her door in time to waylay you. I'm supposed to tell you she thinks you're more handsome than ever." Chuckling, Cybil grabbed both his cheeks. "Isn't he pretty?"

"Don't start."

"Oh, but you are. Such a pretty face. All the female hearts flutter." She laughed again, then snagged Preston's hand. "Come on, let's have a drink to celebrate."

He started to refuse, then shrugged. It wouldn't do any harm to take a few minutes to size up Cybil's brother.

"What kind of sculptor?"

"I work in metal primarily." Matthew peeled off his jacket, tossed it carelessly over the arm of a chair. It barely had time to land before Cybil snatched it off.

"I'll just hang this in the bathroom to dry. Preston pour us some wine, will you?"

"Sure."

"She have any beer?" Matthew wanted to know and sauntered over to lean on the counter while Preston moved through the kitchen with a familiarity that had the big brother arching a brow.

"Yeah." He plucked out two, popped the tops, then took out the wine for Cybil. "You work in the South?"

"That's right. New Orleans suits me better than New England. Weather-wise, it gives me more room to work outside if I want. Cyb hasn't mentioned you. When did you move in?"

Preston lifted his beer, noted Matthew's eyes were nearly the exact color of Cybil's hair. Like good aged whiskey. "Not long ago."

"Work fast, do you?"

"Depends."

"Preston." Cybil heaved a sigh as she came back. "Couldn't you have used glasses?"

"We don't need glasses." Matthew grinned, keeping a challenging eye on Preston. "We'll just drink our beer like real men, then chew up the bottle."

"Then you probably don't want any dainty cheese and crackers, or girlie pâté to go with it."

"Says who?" Matthew demanded, and slid onto a stool. "You used to have four of these, didn't you?"

"Oh, Preston borrowed one. What are you doing in New York, Matthew?" She stuck her head in the fridge.

"Just some quick preliminary business for my show this fall. I'm only here for a couple days."

"And you checked into a hotel, didn't you?"

"Your revolving-door policy drives me crazy." Matthew gestured toward Preston with his beer. "You've lived across the hall for a bit, right? So you know what goes on in here. It's terrifying. She lets…" He shuddered dramatically. "People in here."

"Matthew is a professional recluse," Cybil said dryly as she began preparing a small feast. "You two should get along famously. Preston doesn't like people, either."

"Ah, finally. A man of sense." Matthew aimed one of his quick, crooked smiles at Preston and decided he might like him after all. "I let her talk me into staying here once," Matthew continued, stealing a cracker. "Oh, the horror. Three days, people dropping in, talking, eating, drinking, standing around, bringing their relatives and pets."

"It was only one little dog."

"Who insisted on sitting in my lap, without invitation, then ate my socks."

"If you hadn't left them lying on the floor, he wouldn't have eaten them. Besides, he only chewed them a bit."

"It's all a matter of perspective," Matthew concluded. "And you see, in a civilized hotel, the only people who drop in are housekeeping and room service—and they knock first and very rarely bring along small, toothy dogs." He reached over, pinched her chin. "But I'll let you cook me dinner, darling."

"You're so good to me."

"You ever had Cyb's homemade chicken potpie, McQuinn?"

"Can't say I have."

"Well, watch me sweet-talk us into some."

It was an interesting way to spend the evening, Preston thought later, watching Cybil relate to her brother. The ease of affection, humor, occasional exasperation. He remembered it had been like that between him and his sister. Before Pamela.

After that, there had still been affection, but the ease of it had vanished. All too often he had felt an awkwardness that had never been there before.

But awkwardness wasn't a problem with the Campbells. They cheerfully told embarrassing stories about each other, and when that paled ganged up to tell him about their absent and therefore defenseless sister and any number of cousins.

By the time he left, he was wondering if he could work bits of them into act 2, for a little comic relief.

Work, Preston decided, since Cybil was likely to be occupied with family for quite some time yet, was his best hope for the rest of the night.

"I like your friend." Matthew stretched out his legs and swirled the brandy Cybil had opened in his honor.

"That's handy—so do I."

"A little on the sober side for you."

"Ah, well." She settled in beside him on the sofa. "A little change of pace now and again can't hurt."

"Is that what he is?" Matthew gave her earlobe a tug. "I noticed you two didn't waste any time getting locked together when I so accommodatingly strolled upstairs to make a phone call."

"If you were making a phone call, how do you know what we were doing down here? Unless you were spying." She smiled sweetly, fluttered her lashes and got another jerk on the ear.

"I wasn't spying. I just happened to glance down the stairs at one very strategic moment. And since he looked at you any number of times during the evening like he knew you'd be a lot more tasty than your chicken potpie—which was great, by the way—I cleverly put two and two together."

"You were always bright, Matthew. I suppose it's reasonable to say, since you're being nosy, that Preston and I are together."

"You're sleeping with him."

Deliberately, Cybil widened her eyes. "Why, no—we've decided to be canasta partners. We realize it's a big commitment, but we think we can handle it."

"You always were a smart-ass," he muttered.

"That's how I make my fame and fortune."

"Now you're making it turning McQuinn across the hall into Emily's elusive and irritable Quinn."

"How could I resist?"

Matthew drummed his fingers, shifted. "Emily thinks she's in love with him."

Cybil said nothing for a moment, then shook her head. "Emily is a cartoon character who pretty much does what I tell her to do. She's not me."

"She has pieces of you—some of your most endearing and annoying pieces."

"True. That's why I like her."

Matthew blew out a breath, frowned into his brandy. "Look, Cyb, I don't want to horn into your personal life, but I'm still your big brother."

"And you're so good at it, Matthew." She leaned over to kiss his cheek. "You don't have to worry about this. Preston didn't and isn't taking advantage of your baby sister." She took Matthew's brandy, sipped, handed it back. "I took advantage of him. I baked him cookies, and ever since he's been my love slave."

"There's that mouth again." Uncomfortable, he pushed off the sofa, paced a bit. "Okay, I don't want the details, but—"

"Oh, and I was so looking forward to sharing all of them with you, especially the home videos."

"Shut up, Cybil." Working his way from uncomfortable to embarrassed, Matthew dragged a hand through his hair. "I know you're grown-up, and you're seriously cute in spite of that nose."

"My nose is very attractive." She sniffed with it.

"We all worked hard to make you believe that, and you've overcome that little deformity so well."

She had to laugh. "Shut up, Matthew."

"All I want to say is…be careful. You know? Careful."

Her eyes went soft as she rose. "I love you, Matthew. In spite of that annoying facial tic."

"I don't have a facial tic."

"We worked hard to make you believe that." Laughing again, she slipped her arms around him for a fierce hug. "It's so nice to have you here. Can't you stay longer?"

"Can't." He rested his cheek on the top of her head. "I'm going up to Hyannis for a couple days. I'll hang out, do some sketching. Grandpa wheedled."

"He's the champ. Is Grandma pining for you?" Cybil asked, leaning back to grin.

"Fretting herself down to skin and bones. Why don't you come up? Give him a bonus. And that way we can spot each other when he starts on why we're not settled down and raising a pack of little people."

"Hmm. Well, he has called here a couple times in the last few weeks—hasn't given me a chance to call first." She considered, juggling time and duties in her head. "I'm enough strips ahead to take a couple of days. I do have a meeting day after tomorrow, though, that I shouldn't break."

"Come up afterward." He angled his head when he saw her mull it over, hesitate. "You can ask your canasta partner to drive up with you. We'll have a tournament."

"He might enjoy that," she murmured. "I'll check with him. Either way, I'll come."

"Good." And, Matthew thought, he hoped Preston accepted the invitation. He would love to see Daniel MacGregor work him over.

Since it was after midnight when Matthew went off to his hotel, Cybil told herself to go upstairs to bed. She hadn't gotten much sleep the night before—and neither had Preston. The reasonable, the practical, thing to do was climb into bed, shut off the light and get some much-needed rest.

So she walked across the hall and pushed his buzzer.

She was beginning to think he'd gone to bed, or down to the club, when she heard the rattle of locks.

"Hi. I never offered you a nightcap."

He glanced over her shoulder, back at her face. "Where's your brother?"

"On his way to his hotel. I opened some brandy, and—"

She didn't manage the rest, or even much of a squeak of surprise as he yanked her inside, kicked the door closed and shoved her against it. Her mouth was much too busy being assaulted by his.

When he switched to her neck, she managed to suck in a breath. "I guess you don't want any brandy." Since he was already dragging off her shirt, she returned the favor. "Or after-dinner mints."

The force of need that had slammed into him the moment he'd seen her was outrageous. He couldn't stem it, even with his hands rushing over her to take. Greedy, his mouth crushed back on hers while he pulled her head back to dive yet deeper.

And she strained against him, just as urgently, just as desperately, groaning in pleasure as he tugged her trousers down her hips.

Whatever she had was his.

He filled his hands with her breasts, then his mouth descended, sucking, nipping while her nails bit, arousing points of pain, into his back.

Her skin, like warmed silk, drove him to possess. Desire, a freshly whetted blade, twisted as he moved down her until her hands vised on his shoulder and her breath was only gasping sobs.

Not possible, not possible to feel so much and survive, was her last coherent thought. Then he used his mouth on her, his fingernails raking lightly down her body as with lips and teeth and tongue he drove her beyond reason.

She heard her own cry of shocked release dimly, struggling for air as her system rocked from the hot explosion of pleasure. Destroyed, she sagged against the door, utterly open to him.

Surrender only fanned the flames.

His hands slipped, slid, over her damp skin. His mouth continued its relentless assault, demanding more, still more, until her body began to quiver again. Until he felt her begin to heat and move and stretch toward the next peak.

He left her groaning, traveling back up her body, slicking his tongue over flesh that tasted erotically of salt and woman. His hands were rougher than he intended as he dragged her to the chair, pulled her down on him, lifted her hips.

His eyes met hers, watching, watching as that soft, clouded green darkened and blurred, watching as those long lids flickered, watching still as he lowered her.

Now, as she closed around him, surrounded him in hot, slippery heat, their groans mixed. Her head fell back, exposing that lovely white arch of throat where a pulse beat in wild hammer blows.

And she began to ride.

The pace was hers now, and it was fast and fierce. Each thrust of hips slapped them both toward the dark swirl of delirium. He craved it, that moment when sanity ripped away.

Bright arrows of sensation, each separate and sharp, stabbed through him. The sumptuous taste of her flesh in his mouth, the wet silk texture of it as his hands sought more of her, those low, animal sounds in her throat and the sheer wonder of her face flushed with pleasure and purpose.

He teetered on the edge, struggling to hold on another instant, just one more instant where he could no longer tell where she began and he left off. But she closed around him, a glorious fist of triumph, and, breathing his name, dragged him over with her.

Then, as she had before, she melted onto him. The sensation of having her head lie on his shoulder, her lips against his throat, spread a hazy glow through him. Closing his eyes, he held on to it, and to her.

He remembered what she had said to him before. No one had ever touched her as he had.

No one, he thought, had ever reached him as she had. But, however clever he was with words on paper, he didn't know how to begin to tell her.

"I wanted to get my hands on you all evening." That, at least, he could say without risking either of them.

"Mmm. And to think I nearly went up to bed." With a long, contented sigh, she nuzzled his hair. "I knew this chair was perfect for you."

A chuckle rumbled in his chest. "I was thinking of having it recovered. But now I'm having it bronzed."

She leaned back, cupping her hands on his face. "I love those little unexpected pockets of humor in you."

"It's not funny," he said in serious tones. "It's going to cost me a fortune."

He expected her to laugh, a sound he'd grown to depend on. But her smile was wistful, her eyes soft. "Preston." She murmured it, then lowered her mouth to his.

The slow, deep, gentle kiss stirred the soul rather than the blood. It reached into him, brushed hesitant fingers over his heart and made him yearn for something he refused to believe in.

Something struggled to shift inside him, made his hands tremble with the effort to hold it still and steady. But the sweetness of it seeped in, left him reeling.

He crossed over that thin line between want and need, and felt himself stumble terrifyingly close to the edge of love.

She sighed, pressed her cheek to his. And wished.

"You're cold," he murmured, feeling her skin chill.

"A little." She kept her eyes squeezed tight another moment, reminding herself you couldn't always have everything you wished for. "Thirsty. Want some water?"

"Yeah, I'll get it."

"No, that's all right." She slid off him, leaving him slightly baffled by the sense of loss. "Do you have a robe?"

He worked up a smile again. "What is this obsession you have with robes?"

"Never mind." She snatched up his shirt and pulled it on. "Matthew likes you," she commented as she walked into the kitchen.

"I like him." He could take a deep breath now. Could, he told himself, regain his balance now. "The piece up in your studio. That's his work?"

"Yeah. Terrific, isn't it? He's got such a unique vision of things. And watching him work—if he doesn't murder you—is an amazing experience."

She opened a bottle of water, poured a tall glass to the rim, then drank down nearly a third before moving back to Preston. She didn't notice his blink of surprise when she settled, cozy as a cat, into his lap.

"So anyway," she began, offering him the glass, "how do you feel about taking a little trip?"

"A trip?"

"A couple of days in Hyannis Port. Matthew's going up to see our grandparents—the MacGregors—and I thought I might do the same. Grandpa loves to complain that we don't visit enough. It's a great place. The house is… well, I can't describe it. But you'd like it. You'd like them. Want to get out of Dodge for a bit, McQuinn?"

"It sounds like a family thing." It struck him as odd, and totally out of character, that he should feel so unhappy with the idea of her being away for a couple of days.

"With The MacGregor, everything is a family thing. Grandpa loves people. He's over ninety, and has the most amazing energy."

"I know. He's fascinating. They both are." He glanced back as she frowned at him. "I know them. Slightly. They're acquaintances of my parents."

"Oh? I didn't realize. I told you the rather convoluted family connection, didn't I? MacGregor to Blade. Blade to Grandeau. Grandeau to Campbell. Campbell to MacGregor, not necessarily in that order."

"Don't start. It makes my ears ring."

She laughed, dutifully kissed them. "Well, since you know them and you've met Matthew, it wouldn't be like dropping yourself in on a group of strangers. Come with me." She ran her lips from his ear to his neck. "It'll be fun."

"We could stay right here in this chair and have even more fun."

She chuckled warmly. "There are dozens and dozens of rooms in Castle MacGregor," she murmured. "And in many of them, there are big...soft...beds."

"When do we leave?"

"Really?" Thrilled at the idea, she leaned back. "Day after tomorrow? I have a meeting midmorning. We can leave right after. I can rent a car."

"I have a car."

"Oh." She cocked her head. "Hmm. Is it a sexy car?"

"How do you feel about four-door sedans?"

"It's probably very sturdy, very reliable. I appreciate a sensible car."

"Then you're not going to like my Porsche."

"A Porsche?" She giggled in delight. "Oh, tell me it's a convertible."

"What else?"

"Oh, yeah. Tell me it's a five-speed."

"Sorry. it's a six-speed."

Her eyes widened. "Really? *Really?* Can I drive?"

"Of course. If by the day after tomorrow the icicles have finished forming in Hell, you're at the wheel."

Pouting only a little, she began to play with his hair. "I'm an excellent driver."

"I'm sure you are." He decided it would be much more productive to distract her than to listen to her try to change his mind. He rolled the cold glass over her naked back, making her gasp and arch so that her breasts flattened delightfully against his chest.

"Now…what do you think we could accomplish if we laid this recliner back?"

"All manner of amazing things," she murmured, turning her neck to give his teeth better access. "Did you know my grandfather owns this building?"

"Sure. He told me about the apartment when I was looking for a place. Turn like…yeah, that's the way."

"He told you about the apartment?" Somehow he'd managed to shift so that his body covered hers, distracting her from a niggling thought just beginning to form in her mind. "When did he… Oh God, you're so awfully good at that."

"Thank you. But I'm about to get much better."

Chapter 9

The house The MacGregor built stood arrogantly on the cliffs above a surging sea. Nothing about the old gray stone was sober. Everything about it, from its spearing towers and jutting turrets, to the snapping flag that carried the crest of the clan, shouted pride.

He had built as he'd intended to, on a sturdy foundation, with grandiose vision. And he had built to last.

The wild and rambling roses that would bloom brilliantly come summer did nothing to soften the effect but only added to that sense of magic.

"Stop," Preston murmured, and laid a hand on Cybil's arm. "Stop the car."

Because she understood, and was pleased to see the sight of that fanciful structure affect him as it always did her, she braked gently.

"It's like a fairy tale, isn't it?" She leaned on the steering wheel to study the house through a driving curtain of rain. "Not one of the wimpy G-rated versions, but one with blood and guts."

"I've seen photographs. They don't come close."

"It's not just a house. It's the most generous of homes. Whenever we visited we'd always find something new. Something marvelous."

As she would this time, she thought. With Preston. "It shows well in the rain, doesn't it?" she commented.

"I imagine it always shows well."

"You're right. You should see it in the winter. We always come up during Christmas. The snow and the wind turn it into something frozen out of time. And last year, just at the end of summer when the roses were tumbling and the sky was so hard and blue you waited for it to crack like an egg, my cousin Duncan got married here. But in the rain..." She smiled dreamily, leaning on the wheel. "It feels like Scotland."

"Have you ever been?"

"Mmm. Twice. Have you?"

"No."

"You should. It's your roots. You'll be surprised how much they tug at you when you breathe the air in the highlands or look out at a lowland loch."

"Maybe I will. I might want a couple of weeks to decompress when the play's finished." He turned his head, lifted his eyebrows. "How's the car handling for you?"

"Since you've only let me drive it for approximately forty-five seconds, it's difficult to be sure. Now, if you let me take it out for a spin tomorrow..."

"Even your powers of persuasion aren't going to get you behind the wheel longer than it takes to go up the drive."

Cybil shrugged carelessly, thought, *We'll see about that,* and drove decorously up the hill, parked. "Thank you very much." She gave him a light kiss, and the keys.

"You're welcome."

"Let's not worry about the bags now. We'll make a dash for it and see how long it takes to have whiskey and scones by the fire."

She pushed open the car door, ran like a bullet through the rain, then stopped on the covered porch to shake her head like a wet dog and laugh.

For ten full seconds, he couldn't move. He could only stare at her, through the shimmering curtain of rain, her cap of hair sleek and soaked, her face alive with the delight of it. He wanted to think it was desire, straight and uncomplicated. But desire rarely struck so deeply or had fingers of fear clawing at the gut.

If he couldn't ignore it, he'd deny it. He stepped into the rain, let the wind slap at his cheeks like a teasing woman as he walked to her. And while she laughed, he yanked her hard against him and took her mouth with a kind of violent possession.

For once her hands only fluttered helplessly as the sudden, almost brutal, kiss staggered her.

But she tasted the desperation on his mouth, felt the barely restrained fury in the body that pressed to hers. And her hands reached for him, stroked once, then held.

"Preston."

He heard her murmur through the roaring in his brain that was like the rain and the sea battering against him. The soft sound of her voice had him gentling his hold, then the kiss, before he forced himself to draw back.

"With all your family around," he managed, and skimmed her dripping hair behind her ear in an absent gesture that made her heart flutter foolishly, "I might not be able to do that for a while."

"Well." She breathed deep, hoping to settle herself. "That ought to hold me." And smiling, she took his hand and pulled him inside.

There was warmth, immediate and welcoming.

Bright swords and shields glowed on the walls. It was, after all, the home of a warrior and one who had never forgotten it. There was the scent of flowers and wood, and of age that speaks of dignity rather than dust.

"Cybil!" Anna MacGregor came down the wide stairs, her soft face aglow with pleasure. Her sable hair was swept back, her deep-brown eyes clear and smiling as she held out her arms to take Cybil into them.

"Grandma." She breathed deep, exhaled lavishly. "How can you always be so beautiful?"

With a laugh, Anna squeezed tighter. "At my age the best you can hope for is presentable."

"Not you. You're always beautiful. Isn't she, Preston?"

"Very."

"You're never too old to appreciate a considerate lie from a handsome young man." Anna shifted, keeping one arm around Cybil's waist as she held out a hand. "Hello, Preston. I doubt you'll remember me. You couldn't have been more than sixteen the last I saw you."

"About," he agreed, taking her hand. "But I remember you very well, Mrs. MacGregor. It was at the Spring Ball in Newport, and you were very kind to a young boy who wanted to be anywhere else."

"You remember. Now I am flattered. Come,

let's get you warmed up. Rain's cold this time of year."

"Where are Grandpa and Matthew?"

"Oh." Anna laughed lightly as she led them down the hall into what the family called the Throne Room. "Daniel's got poor Matthew hammering on the pump for the pool. He says it's acting up, and you know how your grandfather is about his daily swim. Claims it keeps him young."

"Everything keeps him young."

The term for the room was apt, with Daniel's regal high-back chair dominating a great space carpeted in scarlet. The furnishings were old and massive, the carvings deep. Lamps were already lit against the gloom, and a fire blazed boldly in the big hearth.

"We'll have tea. I imagine Daniel will insist we add whiskey to that and use company as an excuse for it. Sit, be comfortable," she invited. "If I don't let him know you're here, I'll never hear the end of it."

"You sit," Cybil insisted. "I'll go. I'll have the tea sent along on the way."

"You're a good girl." Anna patted Cybil's

hand as she sat by the fire. "You always were." Anna gestured to the chair beside hers. "Preston, Daniel and I saw your play in Boston some months ago. It was powerful, and wrenching. Your family must be so proud of what you've accomplished."

"Actually, I think they were more surprised."

"Sometimes that amounts to the same thing. We never really expect our children or our siblings, no matter how we admire them, to exhibit real genius. It brings us a jolt, and we think— how could I have missed that all those years?"

"You know my family," he said quietly. "So you'd know the play cut very close to home."

"Yes, I know. Sometimes a wound needs to be lanced or it festers. Is your sister well?"

"Yes, she has the children. They center her."

"And you, Preston? Is it your work that centers you?"

"Apparently."

"I'm sorry." Annoyed with herself, Anna lifted her hands. "I'm prying—and I usually leave that to my husband. I'm interested because I remember that young boy at the Spring Ball and the way he looked after his sister. It reminded me of the way Alan and Caine always looked after Serena—and how it irritated her as it appeared to irritate...it's Jenna, isn't it?"

"Yes." He smiled now. "It used to drive her crazy." But the smile soon faded. "If I'd done a better job of it years later, she'd never have been hurt."

"Preston, you didn't hurt her," Anna reminded him. "And, truly, I didn't mean to take you back there. Will you tell me about what you're working on now, or do you keep such matters secret?"

"It's a love story, set in New York. At least, that's the way it's turning out."

His gaze flicked past her shoulder when he heard laughter rolling down the hall. Yes, Anna thought, that seemed to be the way it was turning out.

"Haven't you given the man a whiskey yet, Anna?"

Daniel stepped into the room and simply dominated it. Size, presence and that great booming voice that refused to thin with age. His eyes glittered blue as the lochs of his homeland;

his hair and rich full beard were stunningly white.

"Is that any way to welcome a man after he's come in out of the rain and brought up my favorite grandchild from the city?"

"Oh, fine," Matthew muttered, trailing in behind him. "When you wanted your pool fixed *I* was your favorite grandchild."

"Well, it's fixed now, isn't it?" Daniel said, and with a bark of laughter slapped Matthew on the back with the affection a father grizzly might show to his cub.

"It's good to see you, Mr. MacGregor." Preston crossed the room, hand extended to shake. But for Daniel this was rarely sufficient when he'd taken an interest in a man. He clapped Preston into a hug with the force of a steel trap biting closed.

"You're looking fit, McQuinn, and a good drink of whiskey always makes a Scotsman fitter."

"You'll have a drop in your tea, Daniel," Anna warned him as she rose to fetch the decanter.

"A drop." For a big man, he could still manage to sulk like a child. "Anna."

"Two drops," she conceded with a smile tugging at her mouth. "Tell me, Preston, do you smoke cigars?"

"Not as a rule, no."

Anna turned, angled her head in warning at Daniel. "Then if I come across you with one in your hand, I'll know who stuck it there before he dashed out of the room."

"The woman'll nag you to death," Daniel muttered. "Well, sit down, boy, and tell me how you and Cybil are getting on."

Little alarm bells sounded in Preston's head. "Getting on?"

"Neighbors, aren't you?"

"Yeah." Relieved, Preston sat. "Across-the-hall neighbors."

"Pretty as a primrose, isn't she?"

"Grandpa." Cybil sighed as she wheeled in a loaded tea tray. "Don't start on McQuinn. He hasn't even been here ten minutes."

"Start what?" Daniel narrowed his eyes at her. "Are you pretty or not?"

"I'm adorable." She laughed and kissed his

nose. While she was close, she whispered in his ear. "Behave and I might tip a bit of my whiskey into your tea while she's not looking."

Daniel's teeth flashed in a grin; his eyebrows wiggled. "There's a lass."

"You won't believe these scones, McQuinn." Satisfied she'd bribed The MacGregor, Cybil loaded a small plate. "I can't quite pull them off. Mine are close, but not quite there."

"Cybil's a fine cook," Daniel agreed, scowling when he watched his wife measure a measly two drops of whiskey into a cup for him. "You've been feeding the man a bit from time to time, haven't you, lass? Like a proper neighbor."

"She made us all a potpie last night." Matthew loaded a scone with strawberry jam. He'd promised to be a buffer, he remembered. "Preston, you want whiskey or are you making do with tea?"

"I'll take the whiskey, thanks. Neat."

"And how else would a man drink it?" Daniel muttered, pouting into his teacup. "So you've had a taste of our Cybil," he added, and watched

with a barely suppressed grin as Preston nearly
bobbled a scone.

"Excuse me?"

"Her cooking." Daniel's eyes radiated in-
nocence. Oh, aye, he thought, I've got you on
the reel, laddie. "Woman who can cook like my
darling here ought to have a family to feed."

"Grandpa." Cybil tapped her finger on her
whiskey glass.

When a man was torn between his drink of
choice and his granddaughter's future, what
choice did he have? Sacrifices, Daniel mused,
had to be made. "What man doesn't appreciate
a hot meal well made, I'd like to know? You
can't disagree with that, can you, lad?"

Somehow, somewhere, there was dangerous
ground, was all Preston could think. "No."

"There!" Daniel pounded a fist, made plates
rattle. "Hah! McQuinn's a good and honorable
name. You've done proud by it."

"Thanks," Preston said cautiously.

"But a man your age should be thinking
of what comes after him. You must be thirty
by now."

"That's right." And how the hell do you know that? Preston wondered.

"A man gets to be thirty, it's time to take stock, to consider his duties to name and family."

"I've got a few years left," Matthew whispered to Cybil.

She merely elbowed him. "Do something," she hissed.

"If he turns it on me, it's gonna cost you."

"Name your price."

"Oh, I will." And cheerfully throwing himself on the sword, Matthew dropped into a chair. "Grandpa, I haven't told you about this woman I've been seeing lately."

"Woman?" Distracted, Daniel blinked, then zeroed in on his grandson. "What woman would that be? I thought you were too busy building your big metal toys to pay any mind to women."

"I pay them plenty of mind." Matthew grinned, lifted his whiskey in salute. "This one's something special."

"Is she, now?" Shifting gears, Daniel settled

back. "Well, it would take a special lass to catch your eye for more than a blink."

"Oh, I've been looking at this one for a while. Name's Lulu," Matthew decided on the spot. "Lulu LaRue, though I think that's her stage name. She's a table dancer."

"Dances on tables!" Daniel roared as his wife choked back a laugh, then continued to drink her tea. "Naked on tables?"

"Of course naked. What's the point otherwise? She's got the most amazing tattoo on her—"

"Naked, tattooed dancing girls! I'll be damned, Matthew Campbell. You want to break your dear mother's heart? Anna, are you listening to this?"

"Yes, of course I am, Daniel. Matthew, stop teasing your grandfather."

"Yes, ma'am." Matthew shrugged, grinned and watched Daniel's eyes narrow into blue slits. "But I don't see why I can't have a naked, tattooed dancing girl if I want."

Much later, after the rain had passed and night had fallen and Preston had slipped into her room to take advantage of her and the big four-poster bed, Cybil hummed in contentment.

It had been a near perfect day.

Perfect enough that she let herself curl up against the man she loved and pretend, in this fairy tale world, that he had scaled the walls of the castle to find her. And love her. And stay with her for always.

"Tell me something," he murmured, too relaxed to worry about how soothing it was to lie there with her arm draped over him, her head in the curve of his shoulder and their bodies sharing a lazy, intimate warmth.

"Okay. Despite exhaustive research, the exact number of angels who can dance on the head of a pin has never been fully documented."

"I thought it was 634."

"That's mere speculation. Nor in related studies has it ever been fully discovered precisely how many frogs one must kiss before finding the prince."

"That goes without saying. But..." He loved the way she chuckled as she shifted closer. "What I really wanted to know—and you would be the handiest authority on the subject—is what the hell was all that with your grandfather at tea?"

"Which all?" She lifted her head, skimmed her hair back from her brow, then rolled her eyes. "Oh, that all. I didn't warn you because I had the pathetic hope that it wouldn't be necessary. The fault is entirely mine."

She shifted, rolling over so that her body lounged cozily over his. "Do you know you have wonderful eyes, McQuinn? They're almost translucent, like I could dive right into that moonlight blue and just disappear."

"Is that a genuine comment or an evasion of the subject at hand?"

"Both." But since it had to be dealt with, she sat up, kissed him, then reached for the robe she'd tossed at the foot of the bed earlier.

"Why do you have to cover up whenever you talk to me?"

She glanced over, and to his surprise, flushed a little. "A latent puritanical streak?"

"Incredibly latent," he noted, but only smiled as she belted the robe. "Now, about your grandfather and his sudden interest in my family name—or as he put it during dinner—the good blood, strong stock in my ancestry."

"Well, McQuinn, you're a Scotsman."

"Third-generation Rhode Islander."

"Hardly matters in the vast and historic scheme of things."

She rose and poured them a glass to share from the pitcher of ice water that had been placed on the bedside table. "I'll apologize first," she said, without looking at him. "But hope you'll understand Grandpa means well. It's all out of love, and he wouldn't have done it if he didn't like you."

Something much too akin to nerves moved into Preston's stomach. "Done what, exactly?"

"I didn't realize it—or it didn't sink in fully until we got here. It should have," she murmured, sitting on the bed and handing him the glass before she'd sipped herself. "The other night when you mentioned how you knew each other and he'd put you onto the apartment across from mine, I should have latched on to it. Well." She jerked her shoulders. "It wouldn't have mattered anyway."

"What, Cybil?"

She blew out a breath, lifted her lashes and looked directly into his eyes. "He's picked you out for me. It's just that he loves me," she said quickly. "And he wants what he thinks is best for me—that's marriage, a family, a home. And that appears to be you."

It wasn't nerves, Preston discovered. It was outright terror. "How the hell did he come to that conclusion?" he demanded, and set his water back on the table with a hard click of glass on wood.

"It's not an insult, McQuinn." Her voice chilled several frigid degrees. "It's a compliment. As I said, he loves me very much, so he obviously thinks a great deal of you if he believes you'd make me a proper husband and be a good father for the many great-grandchildren he hopes I'll give him."

"I thought you didn't want marriage."

"I didn't say I did. I said he wanted it for me." Her chin jerked up before she got out of bed again, stalking to the bureau to snatch up her brush and drag it over her hair. "And the fact that you're so obviously appalled is incredibly insulting."

"I suppose you think it's amusing."

"I think it's sweet."

"You think it's sweet for your ninety-something grandfather to pick out men for you?"

"He isn't grabbing them off the street corner for me to audition." Ridiculously hurt, she slammed down the brush. "You needn't panic, McQuinn. I'm not buying my trousseau or booking chapels. I'm perfectly capable of finding my own husband when and if I want one. Which I've already said I don't."

She tossed her head and, for lack of something better to do with her hand, wrenched open a jar of cream and began to slather it on her hands.

"Now, I'm tired, and I'd like to go to bed. And since you don't care to sleep with me after sex, you should go."

Was it just temper, he wondered, or was there something more in the reflection of her eyes in the mirror? "Why are you angry?"

"Why am I angry?" she said quietly, unsure if she wanted to weep or scream. "How can someone who writes about what's inside people with such insight, such sensitivity, ask a question like that? Why am I angry, Preston?"

She turned then because it was best to face the issue head-on. "Because you're sitting there in the bed we just shared, still warm from me and utterly baffled, completely shocked that someone who loves me thinks there could or should be something more between us than sex."

"Of course there's more between us than sex." His own temper started to twitch as he grabbed his jeans and tugged them on.

"Is there? Is there really?"

The cool, flat tone had him looking over, had the sneaky worm of guilt sliding into him. "I care about you, Cybil. You know I do."

"You find me amusing. That's not the same thing."

Yes, there was more than temper, he realized before she turned away. There was hurt. Somehow he'd hurt her again without plan or purpose. He took her arm, firmly turned her back. "I care about you."

Her heart, already too much his, softened.

"All right." She touched a hand to his, squeezed, released. "Let's forget about it."

He wanted to agree, to keep it simple. But the smile she'd tossed him before she'd walked to the window hadn't reached her eyes. And those eyes had been wounded. "Cybil, I don't have more than that."

"I didn't ask for more than that. The moon's come out. All the clouds have been blown away. We can walk the cliffs tomorrow. It's a little chilly, though." Absently, her heart weeping in her breast, she rubbed her arms. "I think we need another log on the fire."

"I'll do it."

The fire in the fieldstone hearth still burned bright and cheerful. But he took a log from the carved box, sat it on the flames, then watched them rise up, lick, curve greedily around it.

For a time the only sound in the room was the crack and the hiss of wood being consumed.

Maybe it was because she didn't ask, so deliberately didn't ask, that he was compelled to tell her. "Would you sit down?"

"I like standing here looking at the stars. You can't see the stars in New York. It's all the lights. You forget to look up, much less wonder where the stars are. In Maine, where I grew up, they filled the sky. I never realize I miss them until I see them again. You can get along, very well, for long periods, without a lot of things. Hardly even noticing you're missing them."

When his hands came to her shoulders, she tensed, an instinctive movement it took concentrated effort to undo. But she smiled when she turned. "Why don't we go out and get a better look at them while they're there."

"I want you to sit down and listen to me."

"All right." Struggling to be casual, she walked to one of the deep chairs in front of the fire. "I'm listening."

He sat beside her, leaned forward in his chair and kept his eyes on her face. "I always wanted to write. I can't remember otherwise. Not the novels my father had hoped for. It was always plays. Everything was very clear in my head. The stage, each set, the movement of the actors, the precise angle and quality of the lights. Often, maybe too often, that was the world I lived in. You come from a prominent family, one with a lot of social obligations and demands."

"I suppose that's true."

"So do I. I tolerated that end of it, enjoyed it occasionally, but for the most part just tolerated or eluded it."

"You value your privacy," she said. "I understand that. My father's the same, and Matthew."

"I valued it. I needed it." Too restless to sit, he rose to wander the room. "I love my parents, my sister, no matter how little we sometimes understand one another. I'm sure I hurt them countless times with small acts of carelessness, but I do love them, Cybil."

"Of course you do," she began, but said nothing more when he shook his head.

"My sister, Jenna, she was always so outgoing, so easy with people. She's a lovely woman. She wasn't quite twenty-one when she married. Married my best friend from college. I introduced them."

It still scraped him raw to think of that. The first step in the whole miserable journey had been his. Glancing at the water, he wished it were whiskey.

"They were great together," he murmured. "Shining with love, full to bursting with hope and plans. Jacob came along just over a year later. And less than a year after that she was pregnant again and glowing with it."

He stuck his hands in his pockets, moved to the window. But he didn't see the stars. "About that time, my first play was being produced. Locally, just a small theater group, but a place with cachet. My father's an important writer, so that made his son's work of some interest."

"It's of interest on its own," Cybil declared, and he glanced back, grateful to her for understanding his need for that separate legitimacy. But she would, he thought, because of who she was and from what she'd come.

"Now I certainly hope so. But not then, not right at the start. And it was vital to me that my work stand on its own and not lean on his. Part of that was pride," he continued thoughtfully. "But part of it was respect. Whatever the reason, this play, this first of mine to be produced, was incredibly important to me."

Because he turned away, seemed to need a moment to gather himself, she spoke again. "I didn't sleep at all the night before my first strip came out. However much I loved the work, I couldn't have stood it if people thought I was using my father's accomplishments as a stepping stone."

"Some always will," Preston murmured. "You can't let it matter. The work has to matter most, and this play did to me. There wasn't any aspect of it I wasn't involved in—the set designs, the staging, the casting, the rehearsals, lighting cues. All of it."

She smiled a little. "I imagine you drove everyone, including yourself, insane."

"I'm sure I did. The company had a lot of talent. The actress who played the lead was stunning, certainly the most beautiful woman I'd ever seen. She dazzled me."

He faced her. "I'd just turned twenty-five, and I was hopelessly in love with her. Every minute I spent with her was a gift. Just to watch her onstage, saying lines I'd written, that had come from me. Having her look at me and smile and ask me if that was how I meant it to be. The more I became involved with her, the less the play meant to me."

Even now it burned inside him, what he'd tossed aside. And what he'd had stolen. "She was gentle. Oh, and sweet. Even a little shy when she wasn't onstage. I made excuses to be with her, then began to realize she was making them to be with me. We became lovers on a Sunday afternoon, in her bed, and afterward, she cried on my shoulder and told me she loved me. I think I would have cut off my arm for her at that moment."

Cybil folded her hands in her lap and wondered what it would be like to be loved like that by a man like him. She didn't speak because she could see there was more. And what was left still caused him pain.

"For weeks," he continued, "my world revolved around her. The play opened, garnered very decent reviews. All I could think was that the play had been the vehicle that had given her to me. That was all that mattered."

"Love should matter most."

"Should it?" He laughed shortly and the cynical light was back in his eyes. "But words last,

Cybil. That's why a writer should take care with them."

Love lasts. She wanted to say it, nearly did, but she could already see his hadn't.

"I bought her gifts," he continued, "because they made her happy, took her dancing or to the club because she loved to be with people. She was so beautiful I thought she deserved to be showcased. She needed the right clothes, the right jewelry, to be showcased in, didn't she? So why not buy them for her? And if she needed a little to tide her over, why not write her a check? It was only money, and I had more than enough."

Cybil could see where it was going, or thought she could. She wanted, so badly, to go to him, to slip her arms around him in comfort. But it wasn't unhappiness in his voice, in his eyes; it was bitterness.

"She had talent, and I wanted to help her become an important actress. Why not use my influence—or my father's, my family's—to boost her career?"

"You loved her," Cybil said quietly, already hurting for him. "What you wouldn't have used for yourself, you would use for someone you loved."

"And that makes it right?" He shook his head. "No, it's never right to use someone else. But I did. She talked about marriage, shyly again, almost wistfully. I hesitated there. Her career needed her attention. We could wait to settle down. After the play, I told her, after she began to move up, we'd go to New York and we'd both *own* theater. We'd own it together."

Together, he thought, was all too often a word that didn't hold true. "Then one day she came to me, weeping, shaking, so pale you could almost see through that beautiful skin. She told me she was pregnant, and lovely, terrified tears slipped out of her eyes and down her cheeks. She blamed herself, begged me not to abandon her. Where would she go, what would she do? She had little money. She was afraid. She thought I would hate her."

"No," Cybil whispered. "You wouldn't hate her."

"Of course I didn't. I didn't hate her, I didn't blame her. I was afraid, I was shaken, but part of me was thrilled. The decision had been taken out of my hands. I didn't need to be practical now but could marry her, start a life with her."

He prowled now, restless in the cage of his own past. "Money was no problem. I'd come into a large part of my inheritance at twenty-five, would come into more at thirty. Money wasn't a problem," he said again, then lifted the poker and jabbed viciously at the logs blazing.

"I dried her tears, and I held her, told her everything would be fine. It would be wonderful. We'd be married right away. We'd stay in Newport until the baby was born, then we'd go to New York just as we'd planned. It would be three of us instead of two, but we'd be happy. We had a touching parting scene as she left to go back to her little apartment—to rest and call her family and tell them the wonderful news. We agreed to go to my parents after the show that evening and tell them.

"I started making plans almost immediately. Imagined myself as her husband, as the father of the child we'd made together."

"You wanted the baby," Cybil said, remembering the ease with which he'd held little Charlie.

"Yes, I did."

He turned to her then, his back to the fire. But the heat that pumped from the flames couldn't reach the cold memories left inside him. "I wanted her, and the child, and the life I imagined we could make together. And while I was floating on that particular cloud my sister came to my door."

He could still see it, still bring it back. Every movement, every gesture. Another play on another stage. "Like Pamela, she was weeping, she was trembling, she was pale. And like Pamela, she was pregnant. Further along, just showing, so I was worried at the state she was in. She clung to me, sobbing and sobbing, and finally managed to tell me her husband was having an affair."

His voice changed now, darkened, flattened, as did his eyes. "She told me that she'd dashed back home, leaving Jacob with my mother, because she'd forgotten something. They were to be out all day, so she wasn't expected back only an hour after she'd left. Wasn't expected to walk in and find her husband scrambling back into his trousers and a woman in her bed. Her own bed."

"Oh, Preston, how horrible for her." She rose then, wanting to comfort. "How awful for your family. She must have…" She trailed off as it clicked. The scenes he'd been painting for her, the scenes he'd painted in his play. "Oh, no. Oh, God."

He stepped back from the sympathy she offered. "Her name was Leanna in *Tangle of Souls,* but she was pure Pamela. Beautiful and clever and cold. A woman who could act without rehearsing the lines. Who could play a man brilliantly, all for money, for power, for the possibilities. She would have married me for those things, and to give a socially prominent name to the baby my closest friend, my sister's husband, had planted in her. But I was no longer in the mood."

"You loved her, and she hurt you. Hurt all of you. I'm so sorry."

"Yes, I loved her, but she taught me. You can't trust the heart. My sister trusted hers, and it almost destroyed her. If she hadn't had Jacob and the baby on the way, I think it would have. They needed her, and that's what got her through."

"But you didn't have that."

"I had my work, and the satisfaction of facing the woman who'd cut through our lives. She wept and she swore it was all a lie. Some terrible mistake. She begged me to believe her, and I very nearly did. She was that good."

"No," Cybil murmured. "You were in love. You'd have wanted to believe her."

"Either way. We argued, and some of the layers on that perfectly presented mask of hers fell away. I saw her for what she was. A schemer, a liar, a cheat. A woman who thought nothing of seducing and sleeping with another's husband for pleasure and going from him to another man for gain. But she finished the run of the play." He smiled thinly. "The show must go on."

"How did you stand it?"

"She was good, and it was only a matter of reminding myself the work was more important than she was, more important than anything else." He arched a brow. "You think that was a cold decision on my part?"

"No." She laid her hands on his shoulders, then on his cheeks, wondering that he couldn't see the hurt was still there. "No, I think it was brave." Then she leaned into him, held him, sighing when his arms finally came around her. "She didn't deserve even the smallest piece of your heart, Preston. Then or now."

"Now she's only an interesting character in a play. I won't give anyone that much ever again. I don't have it to give."

"If you believe that, you've let her take more." She lifted her head, and her eyes were drenched. "You've let her win."

"Nobody won, my sister, my friend, me. Three lives damaged, and all she got from it was a few auditions. Nobody won," he murmured, and brushed a tear from her cheek with his thumb. "Don't cry. I didn't tell you to make you cry, just to help you understand who I am."

"I know who you are, and I can't help hurting for you."

"Cybil." He brought her close again. "If you keep wearing your heart that close to the surface, someone's going to come along and break it."

She closed her eyes but didn't tell him some-one already had.

Chapter 10

It was time, Daniel decided, to have a private little chat with young Preston McQuinn. It was simple enough to lure the man up into his tower office while Cybil was busy with Anna in another part of the house. And Matthew—well, the boy was likely off somewhere or other looking for inspiration for one of his metal toys.

Matthew's sculptures invariably brought Daniel both puzzlement and pride.

"Have a seat, lad. Stretch out your legs." Daniel walked to the bookshelf, took out a copy of *War and Peace* and chose a cigar out of the hollow. "Will you have one?"

Preston only lifted a brow. "No, thanks. Interesting literature, Mr. MacGregor."

"Well, a man does what he can to keep his woman off his back." Daniel ran the length of the cigar under his nose, sniffing in appreciation, sighed in anticipation as he sat, then took his time lighting it. Part of the pleasure was in the small and delightful steps.

He unlocked the bottom drawer in his huge oak desk, took out a large carved shell and set it in the center of his blotter as an ashtray. Following that came a tiny battery-operated fan. It was the newest of Daniel's attempts to keep Anna from sniffing him out.

"Wife doesn't want me smoking." The pity of it had Daniel shaking his head. "And the older she gets, the sharper her nose. Got one like a bloodhound," he muttered, then settled back, sighed. "Now, then."

"What if she comes up?" Preston wanted to know.

"We worry about that if and when, boy, if and when." But his healthy fear of his wife's wrath had him nudging the little fan closer. "So tell me, your play's going well for you?"

"Yes, it is."

"I'm not only asking as an investor, I want you to know. I'm interested in you."

"Mmm-hmm."

"Admire your father's work. Got some of his books around here." Daniel leaned back in the enormous leather chair, puffed out smoke. "A bird tells me that Hollywood's taken quite an interest in your work, McQuinn."

"You've got a good ear for birds."

"I do indeed. How does it sit with you, this movie business?"

"Well enough."

"You play poker, don't you, McQuinn?"

"I've been known to ante up occasionally."

"I'll wager you play a fine game of it. You're not one to give your hand away. I like that." Contemplatively, Daniel tapped his cigar on the shell. "You'll be in New York a few more weeks?"

"Another month, anyway. Most of the work on the house should be done by then."

"A fine big house, too, by the sea." Daniel

smiled as Preston narrowed his eyes. "The birds tell me all manner of things. It's good for a man to have a house of his own. Some of us aren't meant to live in a hive, with people buzzing through the next wall. We need our own space, for ourselves, for our family. Room to spread out," he continued, gesturing. "A place where a man can go to have a damn cigar in his own house without being nagged half to death."

As Daniel scowled, took another puff, Preston's lips twitched.

"True enough," Preston agreed. "Though I wouldn't say my house is anywhere near the scale of yours."

"Young yet, aren't you? You build as you go. And you'd need the sea, as I did, having grown up with it outside your door."

"I prefer it to the city." Since he wasn't quite sure where the conversation was headed, Preston didn't relax quite yet. "And if I had to live in a suburban development I'd likely slit my throat in a week."

Daniel laughed, puffed and eyed Preston through the cloud of smoke. "You're a man who needs his privacy, and that's a reasonable thing.

But when solitude and privacy become isolation, it's not always healthy, is it?"

Preston angled his head. "I don't see any neighbors mowing their yards and trimming their hedges when I look out the windows of Castle MacGregor."

Daniel's grin flashed in his beard. "That you don't, McQuinn. But while private we are, isolated we aren't. You know Cybil grew up by the sea, as well." He clamped the cigar between his teeth. "Along the coast of Maine, where her father guarded his privacy like a pit bull."

"So I've heard," Preston said mildly.

"Her father's a good man for all he's a Campbell." Idly, Daniel drummed his fingers on the edge of his desk. "Time was a highlander'd sooner bed down with rats and weasels than let a Campbell through the front door. You don't hold the '45 against him and his, do you, McQuinn?"

It took him a minute, possibly longer, to realize Daniel referred to the Jacobite Rebellion over two hundred years before. Thinking a laugh would be out of place, he disguised it with a cough. "No," he said, very seriously. "Times change. We have to move on."

"Right enough." Pleased, Daniel thumped a fist on the desk. "And as I said, he's a good man, and his wife's a fine woman. Comes from good stock herself. Their children do them proud."

At sea, Preston merely nodded. "I'm sure you're right."

"Of course I'm right. You've seen for yourself, haven't you? She's a bright and lovely woman, my Cybil. A heart big as the moon, warm as the sun. She draws people to her just by being. There's a light about her, don't you think?"

"I think she's unique."

"That she is. There's no deceit in her, or guile," Daniel continued, his blue eyes sharp and focused. "Too often she puts her own feelings aside to spare another's. Not that she's a doormat, not with that good Scots' blood in her. She'll spit when she's cornered, but she's more likely to hurt herself before she'd hurt another. Causes me some worry."

Though he was hearing no more than he'd seen for himself, Daniel's words had Preston shifting uncomfortably in the chair. "I don't think you have to worry about Cybil."

"It's a grandparent's right, duty, and pleasure if it comes down to it, to worry about his chicks. She wants a place to put all the love she holds inside her. The man who engages that heart of hers will live his life lucky."

"Yes, he will."

"You've had your eye on her, McQuinn." Daniel leaned forward now. "I don't need birds to tell me that."

More than my eye, Preston thought with an inward wince. "As you said, she's a lovely woman."

"And you're a single man of thirty. What are your intentions?"

Well, Preston thought, that was cutting straight to the core. "I don't have any."

"Then it's time you got some." To punctuate, Daniel banged his fist on the desk. "You're not blind or stupid, are you?"

"No."

"Well then, what's stopping you? The girl's exactly what you need to lighten up that serious nature of yours, to keep you from burrowing into a cave like a bear with indigestion." Eyes narrowed, he jabbed out with the cigar. "And if I didn't know you were just what's best for her, you wouldn't be within arm's reach, I can tell you that."

"You put me in arm's reach, Mr. MacGregor." Feeling trapped, and furious because of it, Preston pushed out of his chair. "You dumped me on her doorstep, under the guise of doing me a favor."

"I did you the finest favor of your life, lad, and you should be thanking me for it, instead of looking murderous."

"I don't know how the rest of the family and acquaintances handle your button pushing, but I can tell you I don't appreciate or need it."

"If you didn't need it," Daniel disagreed in a roar, "why are you still moping about something that's gone—and never really was—instead of taking hold of what is?"

The temper that had been heating Preston's eyes turned to ice. "That's my business."

"It's your flaw," Daniel disagreed, more pleased than not to watch the anger, and the control. "And a man's entitled to one or two.

I've had over ninety years in this world to watch people, to measure them, to see them as they are. I'll tell you something, McQuinn, that you're either too young or too stubborn to see for yourself—you match, the pair of you. One balancing the other."

"You're wrong."

"Hah! Damned if I am. The lass wouldn't have asked you to this house if she wasn't already in love with you. And you'd not have come unless you were already in love with her."

So he goes pale at that, Daniel thought, sitting back again with satisfaction. Love, for some, was a scary business.

"You've miscalculated." Preston spoke softly as his stomach clenched into a dozen tight fists. "Love has nothing to do with what's between Cybil and me. And if I hurt her. When I hurt her," Preston corrected, "you'll own part of the blame for it."

He stalked out, leaving Daniel puffing on his cigar. Hurt was part of love, he acknowledged. Though he'd suffer for knowing his precious girl would ache a bit along the way. And yes,

he'd own part of the blame for it. But when the
man stopped wriggling like a stubborn trout on
the line and made her happy... Well then, who
would own the credit, he'd like to know, if it
wasn't Daniel MacGregor?

And laughing, he finished his cigar in secret
delight.

Cybil was sorry the trip to Hyannis had put
Preston in a prickly mood. One, she thought,
that hadn't completely reversed itself after a
week back in New York.

He was a difficult man. She accepted that.
Now that she knew the full story of what he'd
been through, what had been done to him, she
didn't see how he could be otherwise.

It would take him, a man with that much
sensitivity, that much heart, a long time to trust
again. A long time to allow himself to feel
again.

She could wait.

But it hurt. She couldn't stop it from hurting
when he turned away from her just a little too
quickly, or barricaded himself against her with

his work, his music or the long, solitary walks he'd begun to take at odd hours.

Walks where he made it clear he wanted to be alone, that he didn't want to share with her.

She told herself his work was giving him trouble—though he never talked about his play with her any longer. She imagined he didn't think she could understand the pain, the joy, the frustration of his work or what parts of himself it could swallow. That stung, but she told herself she accepted it.

She'd always been able to lie to herself more easily than she had to others.

Her own work had taken a new turn and was involving more of her time and energy. The meeting she'd had just before leaving for Hyannis had been a vital one. But she'd told no one. Not family, not friends, not her lover.

Superstitious, she supposed, as she climbed out of a cab in front of her building. She'd been afraid to say it out loud and jinx it before it was real.

Now it was.

She pressed a hand to her heart, felt it thud in hard, excited beats. Heard herself giggle. Now it was very real, and she couldn't wait to tell everyone.

Maybe she'd have a party to celebrate. A loud, silly, joyful bash of a party.

Champagne and balloons. Pizza and caviar.

As if preparing for it, she danced up the steps. She had to call her parents, her family, to grab Jody so they could squeal at each other.

But first, she had to tell Preston.

She used the knuckles of both fists, rapping a cheerful tattoo on his door. He'd be working, she thought, but this couldn't wait. He'd understand.

They had to celebrate. Glug champagne in the middle of the afternoon, get a little drunk and stupid and make crazy love.

When he opened the door she was shining like a sunbeam.

"Hi! I just got back. You won't believe it."

He was rumpled, unshaven, and resented the fact that one look at her could yank his mind right out of his play. Just one look. "I'm working, Cybil."

"I know. I'm sorry. But I'm going to burst if I don't tell somebody." She lifted her hands to his face, rubbed them over the stubble. "You look like you could use a quick break anyway."

"I'm in the middle of things," he began, but she was already breezing in.

"I bet you haven't eaten lunch. I just had the most incredible lunch at this new hot spot uptown. Why don't I fix you a sandwich and we'll—"

"I don't want a sandwich." He heard the edgy snap to his voice, didn't bother to soften it as he stalked to the stove to pour coffee that had been ripening for hours. "And I don't have time for one. I want to work."

"You have to eat." She had her head inside his fridge, then brought it out again when she heard him go upstairs. "Oh, for heaven's sake." She blew out a breath, rolled her eyes and started up after him.

"Okay, forget the sandwich. I just have to tell you how I spent my day. God, McQuinn, it's dark as a tomb in here." Instinctively, she marched to the window, started to throw open the drapes.

"Leave them alone. Damn it, Cybil."

Her hand froze, then dropped away, as slowly,

as completely, as her mood. He was already at the keyboard, she noted, already closed off from her, just as he closed himself off from the life that surged and pulsed outside his curtained window.

He worked with lamplight and stale coffee. And with his back to her.

Nothing that was inside her, that had been bubbling like a geyser, mattered to him.

"It's so easy for you to ignore me," she murmured. "To dismiss me."

There was no mistaking the hurt in her voice. He braced himself against it, refused to feel guilty. "It's not easy, but right now it's necessary."

"Yes, you're working, and I've got some nerve, don't I, interrupting genius, interfering with such a grand enterprise. One I couldn't possibly understand."

Irritated, he flicked a glance at her. "You can work with people hovering. I can't."

"Then again," she continued, "it's easy for you to ignore and dismiss me at other times, too, when work has nothing to do with it."

He pushed away from the keyboard, shifted

toward her. "I'm not in the mood to argue with you."

"And, of course, it always comes down to your moods. If you're in the mood to be with me or be alone. To talk to me or be quiet. To touch me or turn away."

There was a hint of finality in her tone that had panic skating up his spine. "If that didn't suit you, you should have said so."

"You're right. Absolutely. Exactly right. And just now it doesn't suit me, Preston, to be treated like a mild annoyance easily swatted aside, then picked up again when you have a moment. It doesn't suit me to have what matters to me shrugged off as unimportant."

"You want me to stop work and listen to how you spent the day shopping and having lunch?"

She opened her mouth, closed it again, but not before one small sound of hurt had escaped.

"I'm sorry." Furious with himself, he got to his feet. She looked as if he'd slapped her. "I'm streaming toward the end of this, and I'm distracted, nasty." He dragged his hands through his hair because she hadn't moved, hadn't stopped staring at him with those wide, wounded eyes. "Let's go downstairs."

"No, I have to go." Because she could feel ridiculous tears stirring in her throat, burning there. "I have some calls to make, and I have a headache," she said, lifting a hand to rub at her throbbing temple. "It makes me irritable. I think I need some aspirin and a nap."

She started out, stopping when he laid a hand on her arm. He felt her tremble and absorbed a hard wash of shame. "Cybil—"

"I don't feel well, Preston. I'm going home to lie down."

She broke free, rushed out. He winced as he heard the slam of the door. "You stupid son of a bitch," he muttered, rubbing his fingers against his eyes. "Why didn't you just kick her a couple of times while you were at it?"

Disgusted with himself, he paced the room, shoving his hands in his pocket, then pulling them out again to yank at the drapes.

The sun was brilliant, streaming through the glass, making him narrow his eyes in defense. Maybe he did close himself off from what was on the other side, he thought. He worked better that way. And he didn't have to justify or explain his work habits to anyone.

He didn't have to hurt her that way.

But damn it, she'd burst in on him at the worst possible time. He was entitled to his privacy, to his space when the work and the words were racing through him.

He didn't dismiss her. He didn't ignore her. How the hell did you ignore someone who wouldn't get out of your mind no matter what else was sharing the space with her?

But he'd been trying to, hadn't he? Very deliberately trying to do both, ever since the little session with Daniel MacGregor in his tower office in Hyannis Port.

Because the clever, canny, meddling old man was right.

He was already in love with her.

If he ignored it, dismissed it, kept pushing it just a little further out of reach, it might go away before it got a good, firm grip on him.

He wasn't risking love again, not when he knew exactly what it could do to twist heart and soul, to wring every drop of blood out of them.

He wasn't going to allow himself to become that vulnerable to her.

He'd get over it, he told himself, and pulled the curtains shut again. He'd put things back on balance and they'd both be happier.

And as far as his insufferable behavior of the last few days, he'd make it up to her. She hadn't done anything to deserve it, except exist. She'd done nothing but give, he thought. He'd done nothing but take.

Knowing work was out of the question, he went downstairs. He considered going across the hall, knocking, leading in with the apology he owed her. But she was entitled to her privacy, as well, he decided. He'd give it to her and take a walk.

He didn't think about buying her flowers until he saw them, bright and sunny in an outdoor cart. Not roses, he mused. Too formal. Not the daisies—they were cheerful but ordinary. He settled on tulips in butter yellow and creamy white.

The minute they were in his hand, he felt lighter.

He kept walking, realizing he'd gone on too

long without taking the time to really let his mind clear. As it did, he thought more about what she'd said in that brief, dark scene in his room.

Just how often had she nudged aside her own moods, her own needs, to accommodate his? The MacGregor had hit that one, as well. It was her nature to think about the needs of those she cared about before her own.

He'd never known anyone as selfless, generous or unfailingly happy in her own skin. He'd stopped being all those things, except when he was with her. When he let himself really *be* with her.

She'd been so excited when she'd burst into his apartment. He'd become so used to seeing her that way he hadn't considered it might have been something special that had put that shine in her eyes.

He'd taken care of that quickly enough, he thought viciously.

And he'd taken her for granted, he realized, almost from the first moment.

He could change that. And would. He'd give her back as much as he took, put them on equal ground. So when the time came to step back from each other—and it would—they might have a chance to do so as friends.

He simply couldn't imagine his life without her as part of it any longer.

He stayed out the rest of the afternoon, into early evening. When he went to her door with flowers he didn't feel foolish. He felt settled. And when she opened it, he felt right.

"Did you get some rest?"

"Yes." She'd dived into sleep the way a rabbit dives into a thicket. To hide. "Thanks."

"Feel like company?" He brought the tulips up into her line of sight. And when she stared at them, he recognized simple shock. "And tulips?"

"Ah…sure. They're wonderful. I'll get a vase."

Just how much had he left out, he wondered, if his bringing her a handful of flowers stunned her? "I'm sorry about this afternoon."

"Oh." So the flowers were an apology, she thought, as she took a blue glass vase from a cupboard. She shook off the vague disappointment that they hadn't been for no reason at all and turned to smile. "It doesn't matter. It's what you get when you disturb a bear in his den."

"It matters." He laid a hand on hers over the tulips. "And I'm sorry."

"All right."

"That's it? A lot of women would make a man grovel a little."

"I don't care for groveling much. Aren't you lucky?"

He lifted her hand, turning it over to press his lips to the palm. "Yes. I am." And for the second time he saw blank shock on her face.

He'd never given her tenderness, he realized, amazed at his own stupidity. Never given her the simple glow of romance. "I thought, if you're feeling better, you might like to go out to dinner."

She blinked. "Out?"

"If you like. Or if you're not feeling up to it," he continued, coming around the counter, "we can have a quiet dinner in. Whatever you want," he murmured, cupping her face to brush his lips over her forehead.

"Who are you? And what are you doing in Preston's body?"

He chuckled, then kissed her cheeks, one, the other. "Tell me what you want, Cybil."

To be touched like this. Looked at like this. "I…I can just fix something here."

"If you want to stay in, I'll take care of dinner."

"You? *You?* All right, that's it. I'm calling the cops."

He drew her into his arms, held her. "I'm not threatening to cook. We'd never survive the night that way." He nuzzled her hair, stroked it. "I'll order in."

"Oh, well, all right." He was holding her, she thought dizzily. Just holding her, as if that was enough, as if that was everything.

"You're tight." He murmured it, sliding his hands up to rub at the tension in her shoulders. "I don't think I've ever known you to be knotted up. The headache still bothering you?"

"No, not much."

"Why don't you go up. Soak in the tub until you're relaxed. Then you can put on one of those robes you're so fond of and we'll have a quiet dinner."

"I'm fine. I can…" She trailed off as his

mouth skimmed hers, retreated, then returned, softly, gently, sweetly enough to dissolve her knees.

"Go on up." He drew her away, smiling as she stared up at him with slumberous, confused eyes. "I'll take care of everything."

"All right. I guess I'm a little unsteady yet." Which might explain why she wasn't entirely sure how to get upstairs in her own apartment. "The, ah, number for the pizza place is on the phone."

"I'll take care of it." He gave her a nudge toward the steps. "Go relax."

"Okay." She started to the steps, up, then stopped and turned back to study him. "Preston?"

"Yeah?"

"Are you…" With a half laugh she shook her head. "Nothing. Never mind. I won't be long."

"Take your time," he told her. It was going to require a bit of his to make certain everything was ready for her when she came back down.

If the hint of romance nearly shocked her speechless, he thought she'd have a hard time forming a single word by the time the evening he was planning was over.

He picked up the phone, punched the button on memory next to Jody's name. "Jody? Preston McQuinn. Yeah. Listen, does Cybil have a favorite restaurant around here? No, not the diner," he said with a laugh. "We're moving upscale. Let's try French and fancy."

He had to grin at Jody's long, three-toned "Oh," then scribbled down the name she gave him. "I don't suppose you'd have the number handy. You do, huh? You're a genius. Now, let's see if you can hit three for three. Which dessert on their menu sends her into a coma? Got it, thanks. Special?" He glanced upstairs, grinned. "No, nothing special. Just a quiet dinner in. Thanks for the tip."

He laughed again as Jody continued to shoot out questions. "Hey, we both know she'll tell you all about it tomorrow."

He hung up, dialed the restaurant and outlined his needs. Then, metaphorically pushing up his sleeves, got down to work.

Chapter 11

She did as he'd suggested and took her time. She needed it to adjust to this strange new mood of his. Or was it a side of him, she wondered, he just hadn't shown her before?

How could she have known he had such sweetness in him? And how could she have predicted that his showing her, giving her that sweetness, would make it so much more difficult for her to stay in control of her own feelings?

She loved him when he was careless and cross, when he was amused and amusing, when he was hot and hungry. How much more could she love him when he was kind and caring?

He was making an effort, she thought, to apologize to her for hurting her. And he didn't even know, not really, just what he'd done. But it mattered enough—she mattered enough—for him to want to make it right again.

How could she say no?

A quiet, casual evening at home would be good for both of them. He didn't like crowds, and at the moment, she didn't have the energy for them herself. So they'd eat pizza in front of the TV, be easy with each other again. They'd laugh, talk about something unimportant and make love on the sofa while an old movie flickered on the screen.

They'd make things simple again. Because simple was really what was best for both of them.

Steadier, she belted a long, silky blue robe, flicked her fingers through her nearly dry hair, and started downstairs.

She heard the music first. Low, dreamy. The kind that set the pulse for seduction. It didn't puzzle her for long. After all, the man liked his music. But when she was halfway down the steps, she saw the candles burning. Dozens of them, with pinpoint flames that flickered and swayed.

He was standing in that shimmering light, waiting for her.

He'd changed into trousers and a black shirt and had shaved off the two days' growth of beard. His hand was already held out for hers, and she stepped down to take it, more than a little dazzled at the way the light glinted on his hair and deepened the blue of his eyes.

"Feeling better?"

"I'm fine. What's going on here?"

"We're having dinner."

"The set's a little elaborate for..." He raised her hand to his lips, nibbled lightly at her knuckles, and had the breath strangling in her throat. "Pizza," she managed, and he only smiled.

"I like looking at you in candlelight. Seeing what it does to your eyes. Those exotic, enormous eyes," he murmured, and drew her close to kiss them gently closed. "And your skin." He trailed his lips over her cheek. "That impossibly soft skin. I'm afraid I've put bruises on it forgetting just how soft it is."

"What?" Her head seemed to be circling slowly.

"I've been careless with you, Cybil. I won't be tonight." He lifted her hands again, kissed them again, and had her heart stumbling.

"I have something for you," he told her, and picked up a small square box with an elaborate pink bow from the counter.

Instantly, she whipped her hands behind her back. "I don't need gifts. I don't want them."

He frowned, puzzled at the shaky edge in her voice. Then realized she was thinking of Pamela. "It's not because you need them, or ask for them, or anything else for that matter. It's because they made me think of you." He held the box out. "Open it before you decide. Please."

Feeling foolish, she took the box, gently removed the bow. "Well, who doesn't like presents?" she said lightly. "And you missed my birthday."

"I did?"

He said it with such guilty surprise she

laughed. "Yes, it was in January, and just because you didn't know me is really no excuse for not giving me a present. So this will..." She stopped, stared into the box at the earrings, two long dangles of hematite in the shape of a dozen tiny, foolish fish. Like minnows on the line.

She laughed, rolled with it as she took them out, held them up and shook so they would clack together. "They're ridiculous."

"I know."

"I love them."

"I figured you would."

Eyes sparkling, she slipped the thin wire backs through her ears. "Well, what do you think?"

"They're you. Definitely."

"It's such a sweet thing to do."

She tossed her arms around him, kissed him lavishly enough to have his blood heating. Then he heard the sniffle.

"Oh, God, don't. Don't do that."

"Sorry." She pressed her face to his throat. "It's just—flowers and candles and silly fish all in one night. It's so thoughtful." But she drew a long breath, blew it out, stepped back. "There, all clear."

"Thank God." He brushed his thumb over her lashes where a tiny tear clung. "Ready for champagne?"

"Champagne?" Baffled, she lifted her hands. "Well, it's tough not to be ready for champagne."

She watched as he stepped into the kitchen, took a bottle from her own crystal ice bucket and began to open it. What in the world had gotten into him? she wondered. Suddenly, he was relaxed, happy, romantic…

"You finished your play! Oh, Preston, you finished it."

"No, I didn't. Not quite." He popped the cork, poured the wine.

"Oh." Trying to puzzle it out, she angled her head as he turned, handed her a glass full of straw-colored, bubbling wine. "Then what are we celebrating?"

"You." He touched his glass to hers. "Just you." He laid a hand on her cheek, then lifted his own glass to her lips.

She tasted the wine, a froth on the tongue,

silk in the throat. But it was the way he looked at her that made her head spin. "I don't know what to say to you."

"Well, there's an unprecedented event." Smiling, he brought the wine to his own lips, tasted it. Tasted her.

"Ah, so this is all a ploy to shut me up." Chuckling, relaxed again, she enjoyed the champagne. "Very clever, aren't you?"

"I haven't even started." He took the glass from her, set it aside, then drew her into his arms. Even as she lifted her mouth, expecting the kiss—expecting, he was sure, demand and heat—he skimmed his cheek over hers and began to move to the rhythm of the music. "I've never asked you to dance."

"No." Her eyes drifted closed. "You haven't."

"Dance with me, Cybil."

She ran her hands up his back, laid her head on his shoulder and fell into the music and him. They danced, swaying together in the kitchen washed with candle glow.

When his lips grazed her jaw, she turned her head so that his mouth cruised over hers. Her pulse was slow, slow and thick, her limbs weak as water.

"Preston." She murmured it, rising on her toes to give him more.

"That must be dinner," he said against her lips.

"What?"

"Dinner. The buzzer."

"Oh." She'd thought the buzzing was in her head, and had to brace a hand on the counter for balance when he left her to release the outer door.

"I hope you're not disappointed," he commented, unlocking her door. "It isn't pizza."

"Oh, that's all right. Anything's fine." How was a woman supposed to eat when her stomach was full of tiny, energetic butterflies?

But her eyes widened when, rather than a delivery boy, two tuxedoed waiters appeared at the door.

She watched, astonished, as with discretion and efficiency they arranged food on the table Preston had already set with her best dishes. In less than ten minutes, they were gone, and she'd yet to find her voice.

"Hungry?"

"I… It looks wonderful."

"Come, sit down." He took her hand again, led her to the table in front of the window, then bent to brush a kiss at her nape.

She must have eaten. She would never be able to remember what, or how it had tasted. Her innate powers of observation had deserted her. All she could see was Preston. All she would remember was the way his fingers had brushed hers, how his mouth had skimmed over her knuckles. How he had smiled and poured more wine, until her head was swimming with it.

How he had looked at her when he'd risen and held out a hand for hers to bring her to her feet. The way her heart had tripped when he'd lifted her right off them and into his arms.

She suddenly seemed so delicate. So vulnerable when she trembled. Even if he'd wished it otherwise, he couldn't have been anything but gentle.

He carried her up the steps, into the bedroom, and laid her on the pillows. He lit the candles as he had once before, but this time when he turned to her, when he came to her, his touch was feather soft.

And he took her, dreaming, into the kiss.

He gave more than he'd thought he had left in him. Found more in her open response than he'd believed possible. If she trembled, it wasn't triumph he felt but tenderness.

And he gave it back to her.

Slow, silky, sumptuous kisses. Long, liquid, lingering caresses. He had her floating on some high, lace-edged cloud where the air was full of perfume and the world beyond it insignificant.

Gently, he slipped the robe from her, the glide of his hands sending silvery shivers along her skin and shimmering warmth beneath it. Through dazed eyes she watched as he drew back, as his gaze followed the lazy trail of a single fingertip over her body.

"You're so lovely, Cybil." Those suddenly intense blue eyes met hers. "How many times have I forgotten to tell you? To show you?"

"Preston—"

"No. Let me do both. Let me watch you enjoy being touched as I should have touched you before. Like this," he murmured, skimming his fingertips over her.

Her breath caught, and the cloud beneath her began to rock. Then he lowered his head and let his mouth follow the path his fingertips had blazed.

Now she was drowning, slowly floating beneath the surface of a warm dark sea. Helpless there, drifting with only his hands and lips to anchor her. And that first wave came in a long, liquid crest that washed through her system to leave it weak and heavy with pleasure.

He wanted to have her steep in it, sate her with it. No sharp flash this time but a slow burn. He explored and exploited every inch of her, lingering when her breath quickened, savoring when her body arched on each steadily building delight.

And his blood swam with it; his heart jolted until he was as lost and open as she.

He murmured her name as he slipped into her, moaned it as she wrapped around him in welcome.

With long, deep thrusts, he moved in her while their mouths met in a soft and stirring kiss. In a slow, sleek rhythm, she moved under him while their hands met to complete yet another link.

They swallowed each other's sighs, gripped each other's hands as they let themselves shatter.

And he was there when she awoke, holding her, as he'd held her while they slept.

"It's definitely number one of the modern-day Top Ten Most Romantic Evenings." Jody expertly changed Charlie's diaper, cooing at him between commentary. "It knocks that Valentine's Day carriage ride around the park and dozen white roses with diamond-chip earrings attached that my cousin Sharon experienced down to a poor second place. She's going to be peeved."

"No one's ever paid that much attention," Cybil murmured, hugging one of the teddy bears in Charlie's vast collection. "Not just the you-know."

"But the you-know." Jody cocked her eyebrows as she fastened Charlie's fresh diaper. "That was excellent, right?"

"It was spectacular. You know that scene in *Through the Mist,* where Dorian and Alessa find each other after being cruelly separated by her evil, ambitious uncle?"

"Oh." Jody rolled her eyes, lifting Charlie up to bounce him. "Do I ever. I was up till two reading that book, then I woke up Chuck." She smiled reminiscently. "We were both a little tired the next day but very, very loose. Anyway—" she shook herself, before carrying Charlie into the living room so he could practice his crawling "—it was that good?"

"It was better."

"No way."

"It was like having him take my heart out and hold it, then give it back to me."

"Oh, man." Weak-kneed, Jody slipped into a chair. "That's beautiful, Cyb. Just beautiful. You ought to write a romance novel yourself."

"But it wasn't just that. It was all of it. Everything." Still giddy, she threw her arms out and twirled in a circle, making Charlie rock back on his butt and clap in delight.

"I'm so in love with him, Jody. I didn't think you could be this much in love and not have it all just come steaming out of you. There shouldn't be room inside for it all."

"Oh." Jody's sigh was long and loud. "When are you going to tell him?"

"I can't." With a sigh of her own, Cybil picked up Charlie's red plastic hammer and tapped the oversize head on her palm. "I'm not brave enough to tell him something he doesn't want to hear."

"Cyb, the guy's crazy about you."

"He's got feelings for me, and maybe, maybe if I can wait, if he realizes I'm not going to let him down, he'll let himself feel more."

"Let him down?" The very idea ruffled Jody's feathers. "You never let anyone down. But maybe this time you're letting Cybil down."

"He's got reasons to be careful," she said, then shook her head before Jody could speak. "I can't tell you about it. They're his own."

"Okay."

"Thanks. I've got to go. I have a million errands to run. Need anything?"

"Actually, I do. If you're going out anyway."

"I'll just add it to the list. I've got a few

things to pick up for Mrs. Wolinsky, and I told Mr. Peebles I'd see if the green grapes looked good at the market. Just let me find my shopping list."

"I'm only asking because you're going out anyway and because it's you." Jody bit her lip, then grinned. "Don't tell anybody what you're getting for me, okay?"

"I won't." Absently, Cybil dug through her purse. "I know that list is in here somewhere."

It took longer than she'd expected—but Cybil found shopping usually did. Then, by the time she'd delivered the goods to Mrs. Wolinsky, the grapes—which had looked appetizing enough for her to buy a pound of her own—to Mr. Peebles and knocked on Jody's door, it was after five o'clock.

She hissed in frustration when Jody didn't answer. It appeared her friend could stand the suspense, though Cybil herself wanted instant gratification. But either Jody had taken Charlie out for a little walk or she was visiting one of the other neighbors and they'd both just have to wait.

Arms loaded, Cybil took the elevator up.

And grinned like a fool when she saw Preston waiting for her in the hall. "Hi."

"Hi, neighbor." He scooped the bags out of her arms, then bent down and kissed her. "Hold it," he said when she dropped back from her toes to the balls of her feet. "Let's do that again."

"Okay." Laughing, she wound her arms around his neck, shifted back to her toes and put a great deal more energy into the greeting. "How's that?"

"That was fine. What have you got in here? Bricks?"

Searching for her ever-elusive key, she laughed again. "Food mostly, and some cleaning supplies. Some this and some that. I picked up a few things for you. The apples looked very good, and they're better for you to snack on while you're working than candy bars or stale bagels."

She found her key with a little *aha!* and unlocked the door. "Oh, and I got you some ammonia—it'll take care of that grime you're letting build up on your windows."

"Apples and ammonia." He set the bags on the counter. "What else could a man ask for?"

"Cheesecake, straight from the deli. It was irresistible."

"It'll have to wait." He spun her around, off her feet, and began to twirl with her.

"Well, you're in a mood, aren't you?" Grinning, she bent down to kiss him. "If your smile got any bigger, I might fall in."

"You'd be better than cheesecake. I finished the play."

"You did?" The hands that were braced on his shoulders slid around to hug his neck. "That's wonderful. That's great."

"I've never had anything move so fast. It still needs work, but it's there. All there. You had a lot to do with it."

"Me?"

"So much of you kept jumping into it. Once I stopped trying to push you back out, it just raced."

"I'm speechless. What did you write about me? What was I like? What did I do in it? Can I read it?"

"So much for speechless," he noted, and set

her back on her feet. "After I fiddle with it a bit more you can read it. Let's go to the diner and celebrate."

"The diner? You want to go celebrate something like this with spaghetti and meatballs?"

"Exactly." And he didn't give a damn if it was sentimental. "With you, where you once took a struggling musician out for a hot meal."

"Did you put that in there? About me paying you? God."

"You'll like it, don't worry."

"What's my name—in the play, what's my name?"

"Zoe."

"Zoe." She pursed her lips, considered, then the dimple fluttered at the corner of her mouth. "I like it."

"Nothing ordinary quite fit. She kept tossing them back at me." He laughed a little, shook it off.

"You look so happy." She reached up, brushing at his hair. "It's nice to see you look so happy."

"I've been doing a lot of that lately. Come on. Let's go."

"I have to put the groceries away, fix my face. Then we'll go."

"Go fix whatever you think's wrong with your face. I'll put them away."

"All right. They actually have places," she called out as she ran up the stairs. "They don't just get tossed into cupboards."

"Just make it fast," he told her, and started pulling things out of the first bag.

He'd been going crazy for the past hour, just waiting for her to get back so he could tell her. Tell her first. And to tell her, to find a way to tell her, that somehow, somewhere, over the last few weeks, everything had changed for him.

And though he'd fought it, ignored it, denied it, it had changed nonetheless. He realized that for the first time in much, much too long, the sensation he continued to feel was simple happiness.

She was right. He looked happy. He was happy. But it wasn't just the play. It was Cybil, and it had been all along.

She made him happy.

It had come out in his work. There was an underlying glow of hope in this play he hadn't intended to put there when he'd begun. But it was just there—shimmering and impossible to resist. The way she was.

It had come out in his life when she had come into his life. With cookies and chatter and compassion. With generosity and laughter and verve.

What he felt for her—what she, being who she was, had given him no choice but to feel— filled him, completed him and, he thought, in a very real sense saved him.

The last line of his play said it, he mused.

Love heals.

With a little time, a little effort, he thought, he had a chance of making the kind of life with her he'd stopped believing really existed.

He reached in the second bag, pulled out a box. And felt the world that had so recently gone rock steady, waver, shake and fall away under his feet.

"I was going to change, but I decided not to waste the time when we could be celebrating." She clattered down the steps at a dead run, the foolish earrings he'd given her swinging. "I just have to call Jody, see if she's back yet. Then we're out of here."

"What the hell is this, Cybil?" Pale, coldly furious, he tossed the home pregnancy test kit on the counter. "Are you pregnant?"

"I—"

"You think you're pregnant, but you don't tell me. What? Were you going to pick your time, your place, your *mood,* then let me in on it?"

The color excitement and pleasure that had been glowing in her cheeks drained so that she was as pale as he now. "Is that what you think, Preston?"

"What the hell am I supposed to think? You waltz in, all smiles, not a care in the world, and there's this." He rapped a finger on the box. "And you're the one who claims she doesn't play games, doesn't tell lies. What else is keeping this from me but both of those?"

"And that makes me like Pamela, doesn't it?" All the joy that had shimmered in her heart throughout the day turned to ashes, cold and gray. "Calculating, deceitful. Just one more user."

He had to steady himself, to calm, but the

slash of betrayal where he had finally, finally, decided to trust was ripping through him. "This is you and me, no one else. I want an explanation."

"I wonder if there's ever really been a you and me and no one else," she murmured. "I'll give you an explanation, Preston. I picked up apples for you, grapes for 1B and several small items for Mrs. Wolinsky. And I picked up that handy little will-it-be-pink-or-blue kit for Jody. She and Chuck are hoping they're expecting a baby brother or sister for Charlie."

"Jody?"

"That's right." Every word she spoke hurt her throat. "I'm not pregnant, so you can relax on that score."

"I'm sorry."

"Oh, so am I. I'm terribly sorry." Her eyes ached as she picked up the box, examined it. "Jody was so excited when she asked me to buy this. So hopeful. For some people the idea of making a child is a joyful one. But for you," she went on, putting the box down, making herself look at him, "it's a threat, just a bad memory of a bad time."

"It was a poor reaction, Cybil. Knee-jerk."

"You could say instinctive, I suppose. What would you have done, Preston, if it had been mine? If I'd been pregnant? Would you have thought I'd tricked you, trapped you, done it on purpose to ruin your life? Or maybe you'd have wondered if I'd been with another man and was laughing at you behind your back."

"No, I wouldn't have thought that." The very idea shocked him. "Don't be ridiculous. Of course I wouldn't have thought that."

"What's ridiculous about it? She did it—why not me? Why the hell not me? You let her jump right back in here. You're the one who left the door open for her."

"You're right. Cybil—"

She stepped back sharply when he reached for her. "Oh, don't. I can't quite figure out if you think I'm just another calculating bitch or pathetically malleable. But I'm neither. I'm just me, and I've been nothing but honest with you. You had no right to hurt me like this, and I had no right to let you. But that stops now. I want you to go."

"I'm not going until we settle this."

"It's settled. I don't blame you for it. I'm just as much at fault. I gave too much and expected too little. You were honest with me. 'This is all I have. Don't ask for more,' you said. 'This is what I am. Take it or leave it.' It's my own fault that's what I did. But I won't be doing it anymore. I need someone in my life who respects me, who trusts me. I'm not settling for less. So I want you out."

She strode to the door, flung it open. "Get the hell out."

Because in spite of the fire in her eyes, they were swimming with tears; despite the fists her hands were clenched in, they were shaking. He went to the door, but he stopped, looked at her.

"I was wrong. Completely wrong. Cybil, I'm sorry."

"So am I." She started to slam the door, then drew a deep breath. "I lied. I haven't always been honest with you, but now I will be. I'm in love with you, Preston. And that's the pity of it."

He said her name, started toward her, but she shut the door. He heard the locks snap into place.

He pounded on the door, cursed through it. He paced the hallway, then stalked into his own apartment to call her. But she wouldn't answer.

He tried pounding again, and finally feeling that everything he'd begun to treasure in his life was slipping away, he tried begging. But she was upstairs, with that door closed, as well, and couldn't hear him as she wept in the dark.

Chapter 12

"I ought to go find the son of a bitch and break his legs, his arms. Then his neck." Grant Campbell paced the kitchen of the home he'd built with his wife, his mood as dark and rough as the sea that thrashed outside.

"That wouldn't stop her from hurting." Gennie turned from the window where she'd been watching for her daughter and studied her husband.

Long and lean, she mused, and still just a bit dangerous. So much the man she'd fallen in love with all those years ago. And so much more.

"It'd make me feel a hell of a lot better," Grant muttered. "I'm going out to get her."

"No, don't." Gennie laid a hand on his arm before he could storm out the door. "Let her be awhile."

"It's dark," he said, and felt helpless.

"She'll come in when she's ready."

"I can't stand it. I can't stand the look he put in her eyes."

"She has to hurt before she can heal. We both know that." Because they both needed it, Gennie slipped into his arms, rested her head on his shoulder. "She knows we're here."

"It was easier when one of them would fall down. Scrape or break something."

"You didn't think so then." Her laugh was as warm as it had been when he'd first met her; her voice was rich and recalled the scent of magnolias in full bloom. She tipped back her head, cupped his face. "You always hurt more than they did."

"I just want to put her on my lap, make it go away." He lowered his brow to Gennie's. "Then I want to rip the bastard's lungs out."

"Me, too," she said, pleased when he chuckled.

That was how Cybil saw them when she came in the room. The two of them standing in the kitchen, standing close, their eyes on each other's.

And that, she decided, that bond, that intimacy, was what she wanted. What she'd been willing to give.

She walked to them, slipped an arm around each to make a circle. "Do you know how many times in my life I've come in here and seen the two of you just like this? And how lovely it is?"

"Your hair's wet." Grant rubbed his cheek over it.

"I was watching the waves crash." She tilted her head to kiss him. "Stop worrying so, Daddy."

"I will. When you're fifty. Maybe." He patted her cheek. "Want some coffee?"

"Mmm, no. Nothing really. I think I'll take a hot bath, then snuggle into bed with a book. It always worked for me when I was a teenager working off a crush."

"During those crises, I ran your bath," her mother reminded her. "Why break tradition?"

"You don't have to do that, Mama."

"Let me fuss." Gennie slipped an arm around her shoulders.

With a sigh, Cybil let herself be guided out. "I was sort of hoping you would."

"Your father needs to be alone to pace and curse your young man."

"He's not my 'young man,'" Cybil muttered as they started up the wide, circular stairs Grant had designed to echo the narrow, metal ones in the lighthouse just beyond the house. "He never was."

"But you're not a teenager now." Gently, Gennie turned Cybil as they moved into the bedroom where Cybil had dreamed her young-girl dreams. "And this isn't a crush."

The tears came again, spurting out of her center, flooding her heart, throat, eyes, as she shook her head. "Oh, Mama."

"There, baby." She led Cybil to the bed, still covered with its colorful quilt, and, sitting beside her, opened her arms.

"I want to hate him." Burrowing into the comfort, Cybil wept and clung. "I want to hate him. If I could, for just a little while, I'd stop loving him."

"I wish I could tell you that you would. I wish I knew. Some men are so hard, so baffling." Gennie rocked her daughter as she spoke. "I know you, sweet baby. I know if you love him there's something in him that makes him worthy of it."

"He's wonderful. He's horrible. Oh, Mama." Cybil leaned back, weeping still. "He's just like Daddy."

"Oh, God help you." With a half laugh, Gennie gathered her close again.

"I always loved the story." Her breath hitched, and she gratefully took the tissue Gennie snagged from the box near the bed. "The story about how you met—when your car broke down in the storm and you were lost, and you stumbled on the lighthouse where he was living like a hermit. And he was so cranky and rude."

She paused to blow her nose, while Gennie stroked her hair and added, "He couldn't wait to get rid of me."

"The way he tells it, you burst in on him. And he was annoyed because you were wet and beautiful." Cybil sighed and studied her mother's face with its honey-toned skin, its strong bones, the lovely fall of dark hair that framed it. "You're so beautiful, Mama."

"You have my eyes," Gennie said softly. "That makes me feel beautiful."

Tired after the storm of tears, Cybil wiped them dry. "We're just wrong for each other," she said at length. "Preston and I. He's so fiercely private, so absorbed in his work. But it's not that he doesn't have humor."

She sighed, rose, walked to the window so that she could see the moon on the water. "Sometimes it can be incredibly charming, unexpected, delightful. He's so moody you never know what's going to pop up. And there's this amazing sensitivity, and you realize he's almost afraid to trust, to feel. Then he touches you, and you're lost. All the things that he is, all of those complicated things he is, are there when he touches you. But he still doesn't quite let you in."

"Good Lord. He *is* like your father. Cybil, you have to do what's right for you. But if you love him this much, you may never be happy unless you at least try to work things out with him."

"He thinks I'm frivolous." The fighting edge came back in her voice, pleasing Gennie enormously. "And that my work is less important than his just because it's different. He doesn't trust me. He thinks he can flick me off like a gnat one minute, and he can't keep his hands off me the next."

She whirled around, ready to spew out more complaints, and saw her mother smiling. "What?"

"How did you find another? I thought I had the only one."

"Grandpa found him."

Gennie's smile sharpened, her aristocratic eyebrows arched. "Oh," she said in the regal tone Cybil recognized as dangerous. "Oh, really."

For the first time in more than twenty-four hours, Cybil smiled.

Preston scowled and shoved his sax back in his case. Damn the woman. He couldn't even play out his frustration. He certainly couldn't work, which he'd proven after spending most of a miserable day between staring at his screen and going across the hall to bang on Cybil's door.

That was before he'd finally realized she wasn't inside anymore.

She'd left him. Which he decided was the smartest thing she'd done since she'd met him. And after brooding over it, he'd figured out the best thing he could do for both of them was to be gone when she got back. From wherever the hell she'd gone.

He was going back to Connecticut in the morning. He could tolerate construction workers, plumbers, electricians and whoever else would descend on him on a daily basis for the next few weeks. But he couldn't tolerate living across the hall from a woman he loved and couldn't have due to his own stupidity.

Everything she'd said to him had been completely true. He had no defense.

"I won't be around for a while, André."

The piano player looked up through the haze of smoke from the cigarette between his lips. "That so?"

"I'm heading back to Connecticut tomorrow."

"Uh-huh. Woman chase you away?" Brow

cocked, André stretched back. "That your tail I see between your legs, brother?"

With a short, humorless laugh, Preston picked up his case. "See you around."

"I'll be right here." When Preston's back was turned, André jerked up his chin, signaling his wife, then stabbed a thumb in Preston's direction.

With a nod, she glided over to block Preston's exit. "Leaving early tonight, sugar lips."

"I haven't got anything in me. And I want an early start in the morning. I'm going back to Connecticut."

"Back to the boonies?" She smiled, hooked her arm around his shoulders. "Well, let's have us a goodbye drink, 'cause I'm gonna miss your pretty face."

"I'll miss yours, too."

"Not just mine," she said, then held up two fingers to the bartender. "That little girl put the blues into you, and you can't put them all in your sax. Not this time. Not with her."

"No, not with her." He lifted his glass. "That's over."

"Why's that?"

"Because she said it is." He drank, let the fire course through him, but found it didn't quite warm his insides.

Delta let out a short laugh. "When did a man take that for an answer?"

"When the woman means it, this man takes it."

"McQuinn." Delta patted his cheek. "You sure are a fool."

"No argument. That's why it's over. I ruined it—I have to live with it."

"You ruin it—you have to fix it."

"When you hurt someone that much, they've got the right to lock you out."

"Honey, when you love someone that much, you've got the right to pick that lock, then do a lot of crawling on your hands and knees." She turned, studied him eye to eye. "You love her that much?"

He turned his glass, watched the whiskey through the smoke. "I didn't know there was this much. That there could be."

"Sugar lips." She kissed him. "Go pick yourself a lock."

He shook his head, tossed back the rest of his drink, then started the walk home.

Delta was wrong, he told himself. Sometimes you couldn't fix it. You couldn't pick the lock, and you were better off not trying. Why should she let him back in? He carried the image of how her face had paled, how her eyes had gone huge and hollow—and how the tears had swirled in them over the heat of anger.

He didn't have any right to ask her to listen. To let him crawl or beg or play on her sympathies.

And he didn't realize he'd started to run until he'd reached Jody's door, out of breath, and was pounding on it.

"For God's sake." After checking the peep, Jody wrenched open the door and hitched her robe closed. If Chuck didn't sleep like a rock, she wouldn't have had to race out of bed before the noise woke the baby. "It's after midnight. Are you crazy?"

"Where is she, Jody? Where did she go?"

She wrinkled her nose, lifting her chin with a dignity that was difficult to maintain in a robe covered with pink kittens. "Are you drunk?"

"I had one drink. No, I'm not drunk." He'd never felt more sober, or more desperate. "Where's Cybil?"

"Like I'd tell you after you broke her heart. Go back up to your hole," she ordered, pointing dramatically. "Before I wake up Chuck and some of the other people around here. They might just lynch you on the spot." Her bottom lip trembled. "Everyone loves Cybil."

"So do I."

"Right. That's why you made her cry her eyes out." As her own threatened to fill, Jody dug a ratty tissue out of the pocket of her robe.

All Preston could do was close his eyes against the vicious guilt. "Please tell me where she is."

"Why should I?"

"So I can crawl, and give her a chance to kick me while I'm down. So I can beg. For God's sake, Jody, tell me where she is. I have to see her."

Jody sniffled into the tissue, but the eyes over it had cleared. And now they narrowed as they studied Preston's face and saw pale desperation. "You really love her?"

"Enough to let her send me away if that's what she wants. But I have to see her first."

What could a romantic heart do but sigh? "She's at her parents in Maine. I'll write it down for you."

Rocked with relief, stunned with gratitude, he had to close his eyes again. "Thanks."

"If you hurt her again," she muttered as she scribbled on the back of an envelope, "I'll hunt you down and kill you with my bare hands."

"I won't even put up a fight." He blew out a breath. "Are you, ah…"

She glanced over, then smiled and laid a hand on her belly. "Yeah, I'm 'ah.' I'm due on Valentine's Day. Isn't that perfect?"

"It's great. Congratulations." He took the envelope she handed him. Then stuffed it into his pocket, framed her face in his hands and kissed her. "Thank you."

She waited until he'd dashed out, then exhaled, long and sharp. "Oh, yeah," she murmured as she closed and locked the door. "I can see how that could work into a no scale. Definitely no-scale potential." Then she closed her eyes, crossed the fingers of both hands. "Good luck, Cybil."

"The MacGregor." Grant said the words through clenched teeth, his dark-brown eyes snapping as visions of murder and mayhem danced through his mind. "Interfering old goat."

Because it was a sentiment Grant had expressed in various terms any number of times since she'd told him the night before of Daniel's matchmaking plot, Gennie didn't bother to suppress the grin. Her husband adored Daniel MacGregor.

"I thought it was 'meddling old blockhead.'"

"That, too. If he wasn't six hundred years old, I'd kick his butt."

"Grant." Gennie set down her sketch pad, deciding the lovely old maple she'd been sketching would be in full leaf rather than tender bud before her husband stopped pacing. "You know he did it out of love."

"Didn't work, did it?"

Gennie started to speak; then, hearing the sound of a car, turned, shielding her eyes against the slant of the midmorning sun. She felt a little ripple go through her heart. "I'm not so sure of that," she murmured.

"Who the hell is that?" It was Grant's usual sentiment when someone dared to trespass on his staunchly guarded privacy. "If that's another tourist, I'm getting the gun."

"You don't have a gun."

"I'm buying one."

She couldn't help it. Gennie sprang to her feet, tossed the sketchbook down on the glider and threw her arms around him. "Oh, Grant, I love you."

The feel of her broke through his darkening mood like sun through storm clouds. "GenviÈve." He lowered his head, took her mouth. His blood stirred and his heart warmed. "Tell whoever that is to go away and never come back."

Gennie kept her arms around him, laid her head on his shoulder and watched the gorgeous little car fight its way down the narrow, rutted road Grant refused to have repaired. "I think that's going to be up to Cybil."

"What?" Grant's eyes narrowed as he shifted

his gaze to watch the car's progress. "You figure that's him? Well, well," he said, and would have pushed his way clear if his wife's arms hadn't tightened around him. "I'm going to be able to kick some butt after all."

"Behave."

"The hell I will."

Preston spotted them as a particularly nasty bump snapped his teeth together. He'd been too busy cursing whoever considered this ditch in the middle of nowhere a road to notice much more than the next rut, but as his gaze was drawn up, he saw the couple standing in the yard of a rambling white farmhouse.

Not really standing, he thought. Embracing. There on the grass just greening with spring, beside an old-fashioned glider positioned to nestle between graceful shrubs, were the parents of the woman he loved.

He wondered which one of them would kill him first.

Resigned, he muscled the car down the lane and scanned the place where he would likely be buried in a shallow grave.

He'd seen it before, he realized, in the work

of GenviÈve Campbell. She'd painted here, he
thought, with love and with brilliance. The romantic old whitewashed lighthouse that loomed
over the cliff, the tumbling rocks that showed
color and age in the morning light, the bent and
twisted trees—all had been pulled together to
form a place and a painting of wild beauty.

The house, with its gleaming white paint,
its many windows and cozily covered porch,
the tidy flower beds waiting for the spring that
would come late to this part of the world, offered simple comfort.

Cybil had grown up here, he thought, in this
wild and wonderful place.

He stopped the car, but the sense of relief
that his bones could now stop rattling couldn't
compete against nerves. The couple on the lawn
had turned to watch him. Even at a distance,
Preston could see the sentiment on the rugged
face of Cybil's father.

And the sentiment wasn't *welcome*.

He stepped out of the car, determined to live
long enough to see Cybil and say his piece.
After that, he supposed, all bets were off.

No wonder, Gennie thought, as she watched

Preston cross the yard. No wonder she'd fallen so hard. Feeling Grant tense, she dug her fingers into his waist in warning. He vibrated like a pit bull on a choke chain.

"Mrs. Campbell. Mr. Campbell." Preston nodded but knew better than to offer his hand. It would be very hard to type with a stub. "I'm Preston McQuinn. I need Cybil—need to see Cybil," he corrected, flustered.

"How old are you, McQuinn?"

Preston's brows knit at the unexpected question delivered in slow, measured tones that didn't dilute the threat. "Thirty."

Grant inclined his head. "You want to live to see thirty-one you get back in that car, put it in reverse and just keep going."

Preston kept his eyes level, unconsciously rolling his shoulders like a boxer preparing for a bout. "Not until I've seen Cybil. After that, you can take me apart. Or try to."

"You're not getting within ten feet of her." Grant set Gennie aside as if she weighed little more than a child's doll.

As he took a menacing step forward, Preston

kept his hands at his sides. Cybil's father could have first blood, he decided. He'd earned it.

"Stop it!" Gennie dashed between them, slapped a hand on each of their chests. She sent her husband one withering look, then offered Preston the same.

He had a moment to think he'd just been chastised by a queen, then his heart stumbled. "She has your eyes." He had to swallow. "Cybil. She has your eyes."

And the soft green of them warmed. "Yes, she does. She's on the cliff, behind the lighthouse."

"Damn it, Gennie."

Before he could stop himself, Preston lifted a hand to the one she pressed to his heart. He could feel his own thundering beat. "Thank you."

He lifted his gaze to Grant's, held it. "I won't hurt her. Not ever again."

"Damn it," Grant muttered again when Preston started for the cliffs in long, determined strides. "Why did you do that?"

With a sigh, Gennie turned back, took her husband's face in her hands. "Because he reminded me of someone."

"Like hell."

She laughed. "And I think our daughter's going to be a very happy woman very shortly."

He let out one exasperated sigh. "I should've gotten just one punch in, on principle. Damn, if he wasn't going to let me."

Then Grant glanced over, watched Preston disappear behind the wide white base of the tower. "I might've been able to do it if one look at your eyes hadn't cut him off at the knees. He's stupid in love with her."

"I know. Remember how scary that is?"

"It's still scary." With a laugh, he pulled her against him again. "The boy's got guts," Grant mused. "And being your daughter, Cybil will twist them into knots for a while before she forgives him."

"Of course she will. He deserves it. Daniel was right about them," she added.

"I know." Grant grinned down at his wife. "But let's not tell him for a while and make him suffer."

She was sketching, sitting on a rock with the wind ruffling through her dark hair, her head bent over the pad, her pencil flying.

The sight of her stole his breath. He'd driven through the night, through the morning, all the while trying to image how he would feel when he saw her again. For once his imagination had fallen far short.

He said her name, then realized his shaky whisper wouldn't carry over the sounds of wind and water. He started down the narrow beaten path toward the sea.

Maybe she heard him, or perhaps his shadow changed her light. Or maybe she simply sensed him. But her head came up, and her eyes whipped to him. Emotions stormed through them before they turned the chilly green of a winter sea.

Then, as if his presence didn't matter in the least, she began to sketch again. "You're a long way from home, McQuinn."

"Cybil." His throat felt rusty.

"We're not much on visitors around here. My father often talks about mining the road. Too bad he hasn't gotten around to it."

"Cybil," he said again, while his fingers itched to touch her.

"If I'd had any more to say to you, I'd have

said it in New York." Go away! her mind screamed. Go away before the tears come back.

"I have something to say to you."

She flicked him a disinterested glance. "If I'd wanted to hear it...same goes." She closed her sketchbook, rose. "Now—"

"Please." He lifted a hand, but when her eyes flared in warning dropped it again. "Hear me out. Then if you want me to go, I'll go. You're too...fair," he said for a lack of a better word, "not to listen."

"All right." She sat back on the rock, opened her sketchbook again. "I'll just keep working, if you don't mind."

"I—" He didn't know where to begin. All the speeches he'd rehearsed, all the pleas and promises, deserted him. "My agent ran into yours yesterday."

"Really? What a small, insular world we live in."

He might have winced at that biting tone, but he was too busy looking at her. "He told her about the series—the television series they're going to do based on your strip. She said it was a major deal."

"For some."

"You didn't tell me."

She spared him another glance. "You're not interested in my work."

"That's not true, but I can't blame you for thinking it. I worked it out, time-wise. The day you came to see me, almost bursting with excitement. You'd come to tell me, and I ruined it for you. I—" He broke off, had to turn away and stare out over the green and restless sea. "I was distracted by the play, and more, what I was feeling for you. What I didn't want to feel for you."

Her fingers tightened and she broke the tip of her pencil. Furious with herself, she stuck it behind her ear and dug in her small tool bag for another. "If that's what you came to say, you've said it. Now you can go."

"No, that's not what I came to say, but I'll apologize for it, and tell you I'm happy for you."

"Whoopee."

He shut his eyes, fisted his hands. So, she could be cruel, he thought, when it was deserved. "Everything you said to me the night you threw me out of your life was right. I let something that had happened a long time ago stand in front of now. I used it to cut myself off from the best thing that's ever happened to me. I watched my sister's world shatter, saw her struggle to function over the betrayal and the pain, to raise her son alone and give birth to another before the ink was dry on her divorce papers."

How could she hold herself aloof from that, Cybil thought, as she closed her book again? How could she be unmoved? "I know it was hell for her, for both of you. No one should have gone through what your sister did, Preston."

"No, they shouldn't. But people do."

He turned back, met her eyes. Already, he thought in wonder, already there was sympathy in them. "It would work, wouldn't it, if I used my sister to play on your compassion? That's not what I want to do. Not what I'm going to do."

He walked to where the land fell off, where it seemed to have been hacked by an ax to form a wall that faced the churning sea. Gulls screamed overhead, swooping down with flashes of white wings, then rising up again to soar.

She came here, he thought, here to this place whenever she visited her childhood home. Came here on those rare times when she needed to be alone with her thoughts.

It was only right, he supposed, that he finally gave her his thoughts, and the feelings behind them, in a place that was hers.

"I loved Pamela. What happened between us changed me."

"I know." She would have to forgive him, Cybil realized as she could feel her heart softening. Before she let him go.

"I loved her," he repeated, turning toward her again, stepping forward. "But what I felt for her isn't a shadow, isn't even a pale substitute, for what I feel for you. What I feel when I think of you, when I look at you. It overwhelms me, Cybil. It makes me ache. It makes me hope."

Her lips trembled open. Her heart began to beat in a quick, almost painful rhythm she recognized as joy. She saw on his face what she'd never really believed she would see. Struggling to absorb it, she looked away, down the long, rocky coast that seemed to stretch into forever.

"For what?" she managed. "What does it make you hope for?"

"Miracles. I hurt you. I've no excuse for it." He spoke quickly, terrified she would tell him it no longer mattered, that it was too late. "I attacked when I thought you might be pregnant because I was angry at myself. Angry that part of me was thinking that having a baby with you would be a way I could keep you."

When her head whipped around, her eyes wide with shock, he dragged his hands through his hair. "I knew you didn't want marriage, but if you'd been…I could have pushed you into it. And my only defense against that kind of thinking, against using something like that, was to turn on you."

"Pushed me into marriage?" was all she could say. Staggered, she rose, walked a few feet away to stare blindly down into the thrashing waves. How was she supposed to keep up with this? she wondered. How had it all changed so fast?

"It's no excuse, but you have a right to know

I never thought you'd planned it or tricked me. I've never known anyone less calculating than you. Cybil, you're a warm, generous woman, with a capacity for joy unlike anyone else I've ever known. Having you in my life…you made me happy, and I think I'd forgotten how to be."

"Preston." She turned back, her vision blurry with tears.

"Please, let me finish. Just hear me out." He grabbed her hands now, gripping hard. "I love you. Everything about you staggers me. You said you loved me. You don't lie."

"No." She saw him clearly now. The exhaustion in his eyes, the tension in his face. If he hadn't been holding her hands so tightly she would have tried to smooth it all away. "I don't lie."

"I need you, so much more than you need me. I know you can get over me and move on. You're too resilient, too open to life, not to. Nothing would stop you from being what you are. You can tell me to go. You'll forget me. Whatever part I played in your life won't keep you from being happy."

He kept his eyes on her face, surrendering everything to the desperate whirl of emotion inside him. "And I'll never in my life get over you. I'll never stop loving you or stop regretting everything I did to push you away from me. You can tell me to go," he said in a voice strained taut with emotion. "And I will. Please God." Helpless, he lowered his brow to hers. "Please don't tell me to go."

"Do you believe that?" she said quietly. "Do you really believe I could forget you?" Amazed at how steady her voice, and her heart was, she waited until he lifted his head and looked down at her. "Maybe I could get over you and be happy. But why should I risk it? Why should I tell you to go when I want you to stay?"

He let out the air clogging his lungs. Even as her lips began to curve, he pulled her against him, kept her there, swaying with relief. She felt him shudder once as he pressed his face to her shoulder.

"You didn't let me ruin it." His voice was raw, and his heart seemed to batter against hers until it moved inside her.

"No, I didn't." She held on, rocked with the knowledge that he had so much feeling for her in him. This strong, stubborn, serious man was weak for love of her. "I couldn't. I need you, too."

He held her away from him, his heart in his eyes as he skimmed his thumbs over her cheeks. "I love this face. I thought I lost it." He brushed his lips over her brow, her eyelids. "I thought I lost you. Cybil. I can't..."

His mouth covered hers. He meant to be gentle, to show her she would be cherished, but emotion raged through him, wild and strong as the sea below them. All of it poured into the kiss.

When he drew back, her eyes were wet. "Don't cry."

"You're going to have to get used to it. We Campbells are an emotional lot."

"I figured that out. Your father wants to break me into very small pieces."

"When he sees you make me happy, he'll let you live." She grinned, and laughter bubbled out. "He'll love you, Preston, and so will my mother. First because I do, then because of who you are."

"Moody, rude, short-tempered?"

"Yes." She laughed again when he winced.

"I could deny it, but I'm such a lousy liar. She took his hand in hers and began to walk. "I love it here. This is where my parents met and fell in love. He lived in the lighthouse then, like a hermit, guarding his work, irritated that a woman had come along to distract him."

She shot him a sidelong look. "He's moody, rude, short-tempered."

The similarity had him grinning. "Sounds like a very sensible man." He brought their joined hands to his lips. "Cybil, will you go to Newport with me and meet my family?"

"I'd like that." She glanced up, her head angling when she saw that familiar intense expression in his eyes. "What?"

He stopped, turned to her in the shadow of the great light with the water warring against the rocks below. "I know you don't want marriage or a house in the country. You like living in New York in the center of things, and I don't expect—you'd like the house," he said, interrupting his own thoughts. "It's a great old place, near the coast like this. Anyway," he continued, shaking his head as she remained silent, just looking at him, "I don't expect you to change your lifestyle. But if you decide, later on, that you want to marry me, make a home and a family with me, will you tell me?"

Her heart did three wonderful and stylish handsprings, but she only nodded. "You'll be the first to know."

Telling himself to be content with that, he gave her hand a quick squeeze. "Okay."

He started to walk again, surprised when she stopped, pulling back so that both their arms were extended, linked only by warm fingers. "Preston?"

"Yeah?"

"I want to marry you, make a home and a family with you." The smile lit up her face as he gaped at her. "See, you're the first to know."

Hope spun cheerfully into bliss. "Sure." He brought her stumbling into him with one quick jerk. "But did you have to keep me dangling for so long?"

Then she was laughing as he swung her off her feet, spinning her in dizzy circles.

* * * * *

Meet Nora Robert's
The MacGregors family

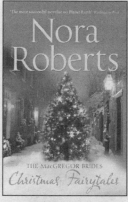

1st October 2010

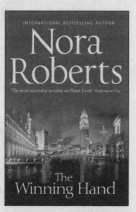

3rd December 2010

7th January 2011

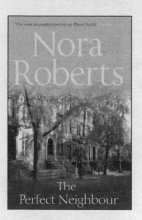

4th February 2011

www.millsandboon.co.uk

Nora Roberts' *The O'Hurleys*

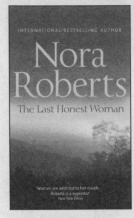

4th March 2011

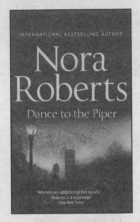

1st April 2011

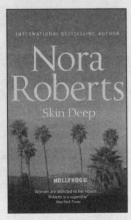

6th May 2011

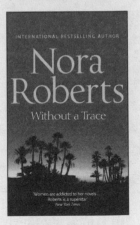

3rd June 2011

www.millsandboon.co.uk

From the bestselling author of *The Lost Daughter*

Laura's promise to her dying father was to visit an elderly woman she'd never heard of before. But the consequences led to her husband's suicide.

Tragically, their five-year-old daughter Emma witnessed it and now refuses to talk. Laura contacts one person who can help—a man who doesn't know he's Emma's real father. Guided by an old woman's fading memories, the two unravel a tale of love, despair and unspeakable evil that links them all.

Available 1st January 2011

www.mirabooks.co.uk